A BOY IN A PARK:
TALES OF WONDER AND DESPAIR

BY
RICHARD PARKIN

"We Are all in the gutter, but some of us are looking at the stars"

- OSCAR WILDE

A·BOY·IN·A·PARK:
TALES·OF·WONDER·AND·DESPAIR

BY

RICHARD·PARKIN

ILLUSTRATED·BY

F·F·WILLIAMS

WINDWHISTLE·PRESS
MATLOCK, DERBYSHIRE

First published in 2019

by *Windwhistle Press*
Matlock, Derbyshire

All rights reserved
© RICHARD PARKIN 2019
ILLUSTRATIONS © FF WILLIAMS 2019

The right of RICHARD PARKIN to be identified as author of this work has been asserted in accordance with SECTION 77 of the
COPYRIGHT DESIGNS AND PATENTS ACT 1988

Printed by BookprintingUK

DESIGN by JOSEPH BRADLEY HILL

This book is sold subject to the condition that it shall not, by way of trade or otherwise, be lent, resold, hired out or otherwise circulated without the author's prior consent in any form of binding or cover other than that in which it is published and without a similar condition including this condition being imposed on the subsequent purchaser

ISBN 978-1-9161553-0-5

for enquiries:
www.richardparkin.co.uk

THIS VOLUME CONTAINS THE FOLLOWING TALES:

The Rhododendron	1
The Heronman	21
The Carousel	39
The Little Ghost	49
The Lovely Red Bicycle	69
The Tomb	81
The Apple Tree	103
The Rose Garden	127
The Magpie	137
The Yellow Frog	151

For my father

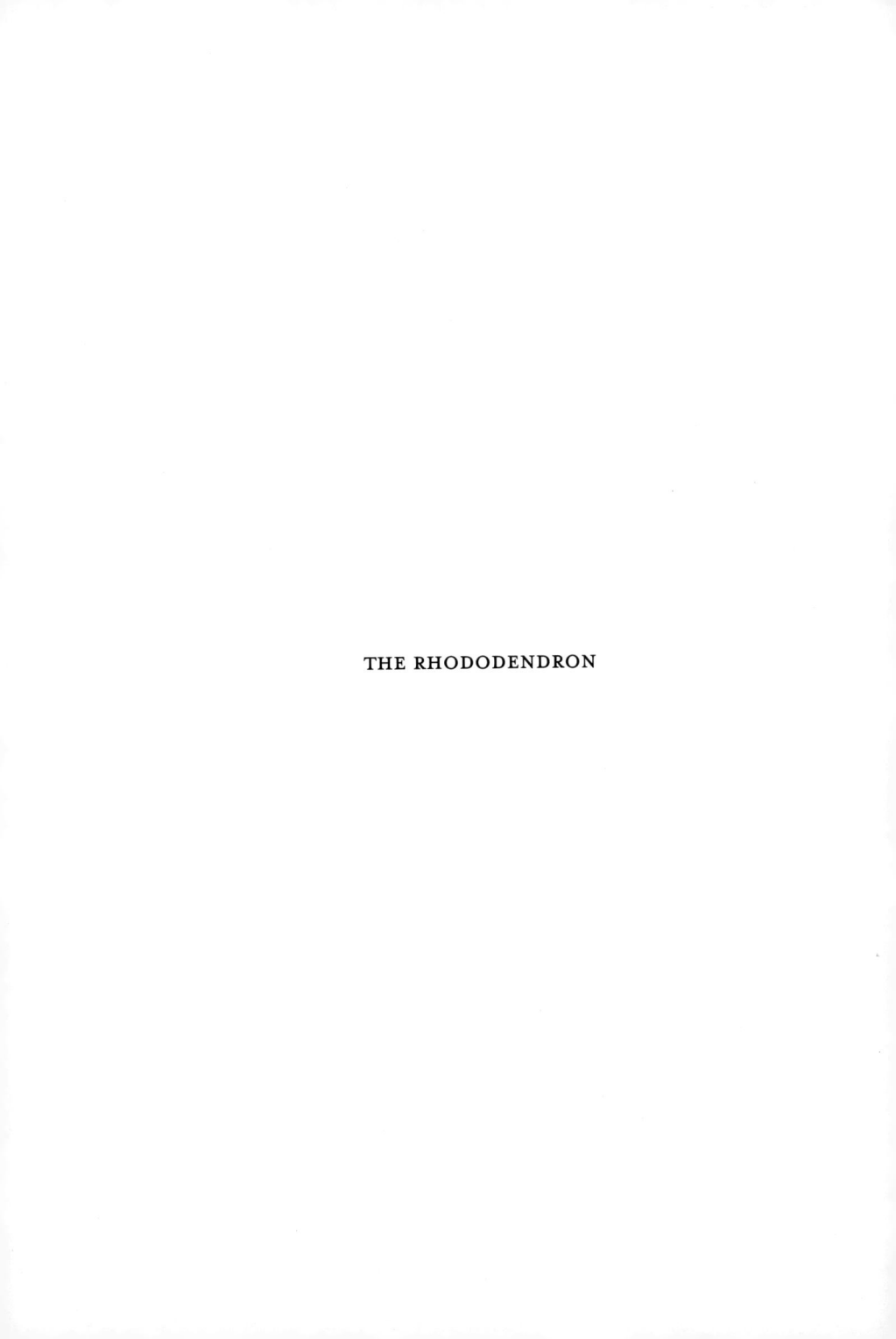

THE RHODODENDRON

Once there was a boy who lived in a park.

It was a very grand park with fountains and gardens and tree-lined avenues. It had once been the summer retreat of a king or an emperor or someone equally old and exalted, but those times had long since passed. The palace had become a conference centre and the royal estate, now open to the public, attracted visitors from far and wide.

The boy only came out at night, when the sightseers and groundkeepers had departed. At night, the park belonged to him and he could roam wherever he pleased and do whatever he felt like doing. If he felt like dreaming, for example, he would take a boat and row to the middle of the lake to gaze at the stars. If he wanted to talk, he found the statues very good listeners. And if he craved adventure, he would creep through the woods where it got so dark the slightest sound would rattle his imagination.

But for all that, for all those diversions, the boy was lonely and secretly longed for someone with whom to share his little kingdom.

One night, while rolling down a grassy slope, the boy bumped into a small heap of upturned soil. It was a surprise and it hurt and he wasn't pleased. He gave the heap a stern kick to teach it a lesson. But there were more heaps. The grass was riddled with them.

The boy knew what they were, of course. They were the piles of earth displaced by moles as they went about digging their tunnels. As he looked closer, he saw how they formed a kind of trail, haphazard and irregular, that stretched across the lawn, passed beneath the flowerbeds and out over the grass beyond. He followed the trail, wondering where it would lead, and whether at the end, he might find a mole busy at the surface.

He came to a sprawling bank of rhododendron and decided to follow the trail inside. The boy was agile and could move quite nicely through the low, knotted branches. But it was dark in there, much darker than the woods, and the further he went, the darker it became. Fear crept up on the boy. When he saw he could no longer see the ground beneath his feet, he panicked and decided to turn back. But he could not go back. The branches had closed behind him and no matter how hard he pushed they would not budge.

The boy had no choice but to keep going, deeper and deeper, until he reached a hollow near the base of the trunk. Here the darkness was complete, but there was also a space, where the oldest branches arched like the ribs of a whale, in which he could rest. He lay down and fell asleep.

When he woke, it was already daylight.

As a rule, he would not venture outside until the sun had dropped below the trees and shadows had swallowed the lawns and gardens, but this morning was different. This morning he just wanted to get out of the rhododendron and he didn't care if it was day or night. He worked his way through the branches as quickly as he could and emerged where a high stone wall marked the boundary of the park. He scrambled over the wall and flopped into the garden beyond.

This is when he saw the girl.

She was sitting beneath a cherry tree, swaying gently on a wooden swing. She must have been thinking hard about something because she did not react when the boy crashed into the flowerbed below the wall. He sat up and gazed at her from behind a hydrangea. He liked the way her hair was tied in a loose bun. It reminded him of one of the statues in the park. Two profound lines creased her forehead. He wondered what she was thinking about.

Suddenly, the girl stood and walked back to the house. The boy didn't know whether to remain hidden in the flowerbed and wait for her to return or to follow her and introduce himself. In the end, he did neither one nor the other. He went to the swing and waited. When the girl came back, she would find him swaying back and forth just as she had been and he would smile and say 'hello' and step aside for her to resume her place. Then she would ask how he came to be there and he would tell her about his adventure tracking the moles into the rhododendron. He would invite her to visit the park where they would stroll through the gardens, visit the statues, and take a boat out on the lake. She would love that.

The boy waited, but the girl did not come back. At dusk, the lights came on in the house and the smell of cooking drifted over the garden. The boy came forward. He could see the girl setting the dinner table. He told himself he would knock on the door until after they had eaten. The thought made him nervous and his mouth was suddenly very dry.

A bucket half-filled with rainwater sat near the door. As he cupped his hands to drink, the girl came out of the house. She let out a shriek.

"Ssh," said the boy.

"Who are you? What are you doing?" the girl responded.

"My mouth was dry," the boy tried to explain.

"What?–no–that's disgusting. Dad!" she shouted.

"No, don't–" the boy pleaded.

"Dad," she called again.

The boy didn't want to run. He wanted to stay and talk to the girl. He wanted to explain. But when he saw her father at the kitchen door, he knew he was in trouble. He ran to the wall, scrambled over and plunged back into the rhododendron.

The boy tried to return to his old routine. He roamed the park at night, going wherever he pleased, doing whatever he felt like doing. He took a boat and drifted to the middle of the lake to gaze at the stars, but the stars were too small and remote. They didn't touch him. He went to sit with the statues, but neither he nor they would break the silence. He stalked through the woods, but his imagination did not stir in the darkness. The only adventures he craved were the ones that would lead to the girl.

He went back to the rhododendron. It was as thick and as vigorous as it had ever been, but if he wanted to see the girl again, he had no choice but to brave the heart of its tangled mass of stubborn branches.

THE RHODODENDRON

This time, he decided to wait until daylight before attempting the trip. In daylight, he would be able to see where he was going. And this time he would bring flowers too. There were daffodils clustered on the grassy banks and beneath the trees. He gathered a huge bunch and set off on his journey.

As he expected, his progress was easier. Easier, but slow. It was hard to hold onto the flowers while squeezing between the branches. He dropped them and had to stop and pick them up, and when he reached the wall on the other side, he had only half-a-dozen good ones left.

The girl was sitting on the swing, as if she had been waiting for him, her head buried in a book. Heartened by his good fortune, the boy decided to make a dashing, heroic entrance and leapt from the wall. But this sudden appearance startled the girl. She jumped up from her seat, dropping her book.

"Hello," said the boy.

"What are you doing here? Get out. Get out, or I'm calling my father."

"It's okay. I just came to–"

But the girl did not let him finish.

"Dad, dad," she called. "That tramp is back again."

"I'm not a tramp. I live in the park," the boy protested. "I brought these for you."

The girl eyed the battered daffodils.

"Weirdo," she said.

Her father appeared in the doorway.

"You again," he bellowed.

The boy didn't want to run. He wanted to give the girl the flowers. He wanted to talk to her. But her father was charging toward him and if he caught him, he would be in big trouble. The boy dropped the flowers and ran. He scrambled over the wall and plunged head first into the rhododendron.

The boy thrashed around in the rhododendron like a wild animal snagged in a barbed-wire fence. It made things worse. The branches sprang back against his blows, bruising his chest, leaving huge welts on his arms and across his face.

Eventually, he blundered his way to the hollow near the base of the trunk. He sank to his knees and began to wail. He pummelled the earth with his fists. The earth began to tremble. Feeling the vibrations, the boy paused. Moments later, he heard a voice.

"Do you have to make so much noise?" it said.

The boy held his breath, unsure if he had heard a voice or merely imagined it.

"Are you still there?" the voice continued.

It was dark in the hollow, but if he squinted hard the boy could just make out the shape of a creature, its snout and paws poking out of the ground.

"Yes. I'm still here," he replied.

"Good," the creature replied. "Come closer."

The boy leant forward warily. He could feel the creature more than he could see it. He felt its clammy breath on his face. It smelt of worms. Suddenly, he felt its paw on his cheek. He dared not move as the claws gently scraped his face.

"You're bleeding," the creature observed.

"Why have you come here?"

"I don't know."

"You do know and you will tell me."

"It doesn't matter any more."

"It mattered very much a moment ago when you were hitting the ground and making that damned racket."

"You're a mole, aren't you?" the boy asked.

"And you are a boy," the mole countered. "Angry, frustrated, upset. Why?"

"I met a girl," the boy began.

"Ha! Interesting. And you like her?"

"Yes. But I don't think she likes me. She called me a tramp and a weirdo and set her father on me."

"And now you want revenge."

"No!"

"Are you sure? She treats you as if you were a monster, but you are not a monster, are you?"

"No, but–I just want to talk to her. That's all. I just want her to like me."

"Pah!" the mole let out a snort of derision so violent it spattered the boy with flecks of mucus and soil. "Enough of this. What do you really want? Tell me, or I won't be able to help you."

"You'll help me?"

"Why do you think I'm talking to you?"

The boy thought hard.

"I'd like her to come with me. To the park."

"Yes," the mole responded, expecting more.

"To follow me."

"Better."

"I want her to love me. That's what I want. I want her to love me with all her heart."

"Perfect," cried the mole. It seemed to be pleased with that answer. "It won't be easy, but it can be done."

"Really?"

"But you will have to do something for me in

return. You will have to bring me worms. Plenty of them. Is that a deal?"

"Yes, yes, yes," he replied.

The boy got up early the next day to watch the blackbirds as they pulled worms from the earth. He noted how they pecked beneath rocks and leaves, but when he looked there he found only slugs. He needed worms.

The groundkeepers arrived and the boy watched them instead. When one happened to dig up a worm, he asked if he could see it and he popped it in his pocket when they weren't looking. He wondered if they knew the best place to find them. In the ground, they joked. And then they suggested places where the ground was wet, near the lake, or some of the boggy parts of the woods. He borrowed a spade and ran off.

By late afternoon, the boy had a collected a bulging pocketful of worms. He made his way to the hollow in the rhododendron and waited. Soon the earth began to tremble, the soil began to froth, and the mole's paws and twitching snout emerged from below. The creature did not greet the boy, but immediately set about its dinner of worms. The boy had to listen to it slurp and snort and gurgle. It was disgusting. Then the mole shuffled back to its hole and disappeared. The boy was outraged.

"Hey," he cried out.

A few moments later, the mole resurfaced with a small dark object in its paw no bigger than a rhododendron bud.

"Take it," the mole said.

"What is it?"

"It's the girl's heart," the mole replied. "It's not very big."

The boy dropped the object.

"Careful. You must look after it. You're its keeper," the mole admonished him.

"Is she dead?" the boy asked.

"She's very much alive and she'll be thinking of you, nothing but you."

"But you took her heart?"

"Oh, people can live without their hearts, a lot of people do. Don't worry yourself about that. For as long as you are in possession of her heart, the girl will want to be near you. She will suffer if she is separated from you. But you will no longer be a monster in her eyes. Just the opposite. You will be a hero, a saviour, a protector."

"But is it true?"

"You'll see."

The boy cupped the girl's heart in his hands. It was the most precious object he'd ever held and he promised himself he would take care of it. But would it really make her love him? He slipped the object into his pocket, though not the one which had carried the cargo of earthworms, and set off through the rhododendron.

As soon as he reached the boundary wall, he heard her voice. She was waiting for him.

"Is that you?" she called breathlessly. "Please let it be you."

"It's me," the boy replied as he crested the wall.

"Oh, thank god," the girl sighed. "Thank god. I didn't think you'd ever come back. I was so mean to you. I thought I was going to die."

"I am here now," he declared with a flourish and leapt down to the garden. The girl threw her arms around him and squeezed him so tight he gasped for air.

This was how it should be, thought the boy.

Over her shoulder, he noticed a small heap of upturned soil in the middle of the lawn.

"Quick," said the girl, sensing movement in the house. "We can't stay here. My dad will kill you if he finds you."

"Where should we go?" the boy replied.

"Over the wall. Didn't you say you lived in the park? Come on, hurry."

The boy helped the girl over the wall and led her through the rhododendron, which was now deep in shadow. He recounted how he had fought through this tangle to reach her that first night–or was it day? He wasn't sure. They stopped at the hollow to rest. She placed her hand on his cheek and discovered the scabs from the wounds the rhododendron branches had inflicted. She asked if they hurt. They didn't–not with her hands laid upon them. It was the most beautiful moment the boy could remember, but it would be succeeded by many more before the night was done.

Together, they toured his estate. They strolled the tree-lined avenues and ornamental gardens, dipped in the fountains, and scaled the grand steps to visit the pavilion with its exotic plants. He introduced her to the statues, claiming them as his best friends. She was right, she laughed, he really was a weirdo. He told her she looked exactly like a statue of Venus only with different clothes. She did not see the resemblance, but felt it was a compliment.

She was cold, she said, and snuggled close to him. He noticed she preferred to be on the side where he kept her heart. He put his arm around her. It was what they both wanted.

The clouds had parted to reveal a glinting crescent moon.

"We should take a boat out on the lake," the boy suggested.

"Are we allowed?" the girl worried.

"Of course," the boy replied. "I live here. I told you. This place belongs to me."

"But you don't really live here," she continued.

"Where else would I live?"

"But how?"

The girl seemed utterly enamoured, but still he did not dare tell her about the practical details of his life. There would be time yet for all that, he thought, and maybe it would all change now he had someone with whom to share his journey.

The boy rowed to the middle of the lake and put up oars. Then he took the girl in his arms and they lay together and gazed at the vast sky above them, the stars ancient and eternal.

"I'm so happy," the girl sighed.

"Me too," the boy whispered.

The boy and girl lay for what seemed like hours, so close it was difficult to tell where one began and the other ended; the only sound the lapping of the water on the boat's wooden hull. But then, quite without warning, the girl sat up.

"What is it?" the boy asked.

"It's my father," she said. "I heard his voice."

"But you can't hear him from here."

"I can. He's in the park."

Then they both heard the voices. There were flashlights coming through the trees. Her father was rich and influential and had quickly raised a search party. It was already approaching the lake. The lovers hunkered down in the boat. The search party passed by. The beams of the flashlights trained on the land not the water. The boy and girl clutched each other tight, as if the strength applied now would help keep them together later, when adversity came.

"You mustn't let them take me," the girl said.

"I won't. I promise," the boy replied.

"I mean it," she repeated.

Their whispers were cut short by a shout from the lakeside. The search party had spotted the lovers' boat and was launching one of their own to investigate. There was no time to lose. The boy sat up and began to row. They were grown men; they would catch him. But with a head start, he might reach land first.

"Hurry," the girl implored, but the boy didn't need to be told.

The pursuers were almost alongside. The girl stood up and yelled at them–as if the force of her voice alone could repel them.

"Leave us alone," she shouted.

"Quick. Jump," said the boy, as their boat reached shore.

The girl scrambled up the bank. Had she run off straight away, she might have escaped. But she hesitated, already feeling the pain of separation. Her father came and grabbed hold of her arm. She twisted and writhed and demanded he let go. But he would not let her go. He dragged her away. She screamed, howled with pain as if her body were being torn to pieces.

In the confusion, the boy sprang from the boat and fled. Only when he'd reached the trees did he turn and look back. Two groundkeepers were following him; the others were helping subdue the girl, who fought them off as if they were devils trying to carry her to hell. Her screams echoed across the park.

The boy ran to the rhododendron. He would be safe there. Its hostile, tangled branches would repel those who did not know how it could be traversed. He clambered through to the hollow and immediately began to pound the earth to raise the mole.

The earth began to tremble, the soil frothed, and, somewhere in the pitch black, the mole emerged.

"Are you there?" the boy asked.

"What is it?" the mole began–it was not in a good mood. "Get on with it."

"I need your help. It worked. The heart worked. But her father came and dragged her away."

"Understandable," the mole replied. "And?"

"You have to help me."

"To do what?"

"To get her back. To rescue her. Didn't you hear her screams?"

"There's nothing I can do."

"There must be."

"No."

"I'll bring worms."

"It's not a matter of worms. You could bury me in a mountain of worms. I don't do rescues."

"But she is suffering. She's in pain. I can't stand it. I can't stand it."

"That was the idea, wasn't it? That's what you wanted. For her to follow you, to need you, to suffer when you were apart."

"I didn't want her to suffer."

"Pah!"

"I didn't. Not like this. It was like she was being torn to pieces."

"Oh, she will get over it. I shouldn't worry about that. She will grow cold and cautious and cynical, that's all. And she will likely never love again. Think about that. In her life, she will have loved only you. Only you. That's something, isn't it?"

"You're a monster," the boy shouted.

"And you are a fool," the mole hissed, and then it shuffled back into the ground.

At first light, the boy crawled out of the rhododendron. He climbed the wall and crossed the garden to the house. He wondered if the girl's father had brought her home or taken her away somewhere. If he had taken her elsewhere, there was nothing to be done. He threw a handful of soil at a window on the first floor. He threw another handful, just to be sure, and then the girl appeared. She looked as if she had fallen apart and been put back together in the dark.

"I knew you'd come," she said.

"Can you come down? I need to talk to you," the boy asked.

"I'm locked in," she said. "But the key is in the lock. Come and let me out. Rescue me."

"What about your father?"

"I don't know. He's gone to bed, I think."

She told him where the spare key was kept and the boy let himself in. He tiptoed across the kitchen. The house was alive with the menacing hum of appliances. He was used to the sound of roosting birds, the wind in the trees, not houses and their buzzing traps. With every step, he imagined he would trigger an alarm. He reached the stairs and began to climb. There was a light in the room at the end of the hall. Neared was the room with a key in its lock–the girl's room.

The girl was busy packing a small rucksack. She rushed to the boy and threw her arms around him.

"Oh my god, I missed you so much. I thought I was going to die," she murmured. "But we have to hurry. My father will be up early and he'll come to check on me sooner or later."

She stuffed the last items into the rucksack. Her face was pale and there were dark rings around her eyes, but she brimmed with renewed energy. She seemed determined. Perhaps if they stayed close, they could have a life together. Perhaps they could escape her father and find another place to live, another park. But that is not why the boy had come.

"I have something that belongs to you," he said, opening his palm to reveal the girl's heart.

The girl eyed the small, dark object. It looked like a shrivelled rhododendron bud.

"What is it?" she asked.

"It's your heart," the boy replied softly. "Please take it."

The girl gasped, half in shock, half in disbelief, but did as the boy had asked. As soon as she had taken hold of the heart, her manner changed completely. Her forehead wrinkled and hardened.

"How did you get in here? You're not supposed to be here," she snarled at the boy.

"Sorry," he whispered.

"Get out, before I call my father."

The boy didn't want to run. He wanted to stay and explain what had happened. But he could see the girl didn't want him there. Any second she would call her father and he would be in big trouble. So he turned and ran. He ran down the stairs, through the kitchen, across the garden. He scrambled over the wall and disappeared into the rhododendron.

THE HERONMAN

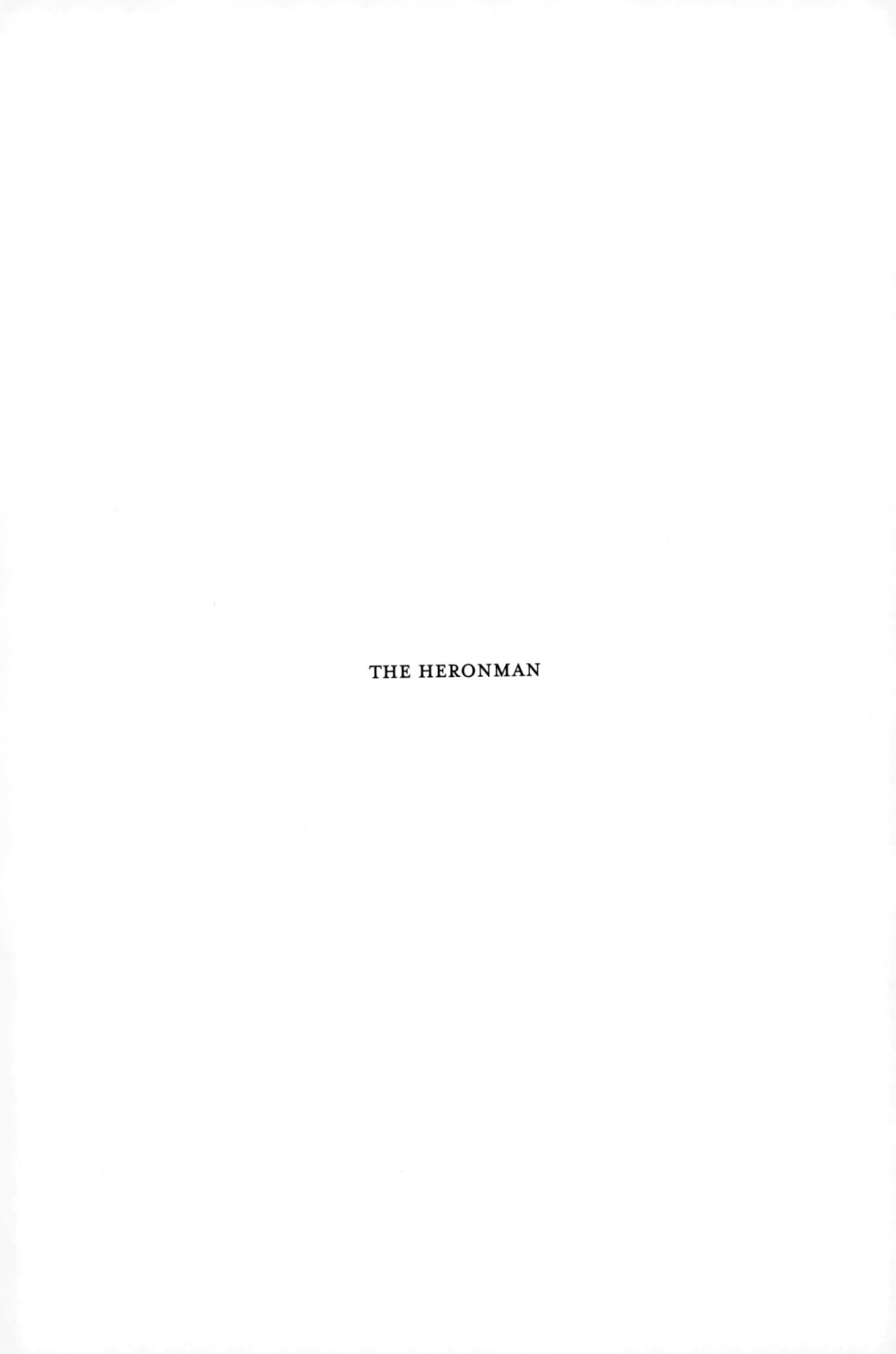

Once there was a boy who lived in a park.

The boy was wild and energetic and liked nothing more than to charge around playing football with the kids who stopped by after school. He wasn't a skilled footballer. He could kick the ball a long way–sometimes in the right direction–but never seemed able to keep it under control. What he lacked in skill, he made up with effort and enthusiasm. He tried hard and practiced for hours with a deflated ball he'd found in the bushes.

One day, he was playing on his own when he gave the ball an almighty hoof that sent it sailing through the trees toward the pond in the corner of the park. He immediately set out to retrieve it, but he found the ball had landed in the water and nestled among the reeds that spread across half the pond. He glared at the ball, knowing he would not be able to get it back, not without getting his feet wet.

Eventually, he settled on a solution. He would use a reed to guide the ball to shore. But when he went to break one, the reed–or rather, the one next to it–turned to look at him. The boy let out a yelp of surprise. He'd been there for several minutes and had not noticed the heron standing poised and upright among the reeds.

A BOY IN A PARK

The heron eyed the boy. The boy stared back.

'What was it doing?' he wondered. 'Why was it just standing there? Why didn't it fly away?'

The boy took a step towards the bird. The bird didn't move. He took another and it merely tilted its head to keep a yellow eye trained on him. He advanced again. He was getting close, close enough to leap on the bird and subdue it. Then, as if it had made the same calculation, the heron decided it was time to move. It spread its wings–so much wider then the boy expected– and launched into the air. Within seconds, the heron had cleared the treetops.

The boy charged after it.

It was summer and the trees were in full leaf. As he ran, the boy caught only glimpses of the heron against the blue sky. It crossed the park and looped around to settle on the iron bridge over the railway. The boy smiled. He liked this game. He tiptoed onto the bridge, keeping low, hoping the bird would not see him, but it did see him and took to the air when he got close.

The boy ran after it once more.

The heron skimmed the slate rooftops of the quiet residential streets, while the boy footed the pavements below, his steps quick and light, thrilled by the chase. The bird seemed to wait for him when he paused to cross the busy road, but when he reached the big park on the edge of the city centre, it left him behind, sailing high above the lake to the trees beyond.

It was then the boy realised what had happened. He stopped short, bewildered, visitors passing on all sides. Strolling, chatting, running, eating ice cream. He was a long way from home, but there was no turning back now. He followed the heron's path and discovered it again, perched on the lowest bough of a floppy-leafed horse chestnut.

"Got you," he breathed as he crept forward.

But then he spotted another heron on the grass further beyond and yet another in the branches of the trees opposite. In fact, now he stopped to look, there were herons everywhere and at their centre, sitting poised and upright on a bench, was an old man in a long coat and trilby hat.

The old man seemed to exert a mysterious power over the herons and the boy too found himself captivated. The man's movements were precise and expressive, like those of an orchestra conductor or a magician. He raised his arm with a slow, magisterial gesture, which seemed to mark the beginning of a performance. The gesture brought one of the herons to the ground in front of the bench. The old man nodded and made a clicking noise. The bird turned its head and the man lifted his arm once more to summon the bird to the bench. With a gentle beat of its wings, the heron landed on the back of the bench where it assumed a pose as serene as a marble statue.

The old man visited the park every day and the boy came to watch and study him. He wanted those powers for himself. He copied his gestures, learned to imitate the clicking sound. He gleaned as much as he could–from his hiding place behind the chestnut tree–and when he thought he was ready, he found a bench, at the opposite end of the lake, and tried out his skills.

But however much the boy clicked and gestured, and gestured and clicked, he could not summon the attention of a single bird, not a heron, nor a goose, a duck, or even the tiniest of sparrows. An old woman further up the path was getting more attention with a bag of stale bread. Ducks and pigeons flocked at her feet. He went to sit close to the woman and soon a pigeon came bobbing toward him. He raised his arm and fixed it with his gaze, but the bird would not stop bobbing and looking for crumbs. He tried the clicking noise and the pigeon looked up. Using a smooth, expansive gesture, he invited the bird to the bench, but the pigeon returned its bobbing attention to the ground.

The boy tried to summon another pigeon to the bench. This time the bird complied, but once there, it would not stay still, as the herons had done. It kept poking around, looking for food on the wooden slats.

"Stop it," the boy commanded, but the pigeon was not going to respond to verbal commands any more than gestures. He shoved it away angrily.

"Stupid bird," he muttered.

It was then the old man stepped forward. He was tall, even taller in the long coat and trilby, and he loomed over the boy, his face grey and solemn.

"Come with me," he said with the same imperious gesture he'd used on the herons and strode off without waiting for an answer.

The boy was sure he was going to be punished for daring to imitate the man. He wanted to defy him. And yet he found he was already hurrying after him. The man led the boy to the bench he used for his performances. He invited him to sit.

"I see you've learned my gestures," the man observed.

"Sorry," the boy replied quietly, flinching in expectation of harsh judgment.

"No, no. You did well," the man replied, to the boy's surprised. "But you forgot the key ingredient."

He handed the boy a white paper package.

"Open it," he said.

The boy opened the package. Inside, he found chunky off-cuts of haddock, herring, and mackerel.

"It's very simple. Herons like fish," the old man explained.

"I can't afford fish," the boy responded.

"Forget about that," the man dismissed the boy's concerns as if they would no longer exist. "Now. Show me what you can do."

The blood rose to the boy's cheeks.

"Now?" he asked.

"Now."

"But I can't."

The boy lifted a chunk of herring from the package. The flesh quivered as the boy's hand shook with nerves. He extended his arm to display the fish, then tossed it to the ground. He fixed one of the herons with his gaze and invited it to eat with the same smooth, expansive gesture the man had used. But the bird did not respond. The boy repeated the invitation. Still the heron would not move. He turned to the man, a flash of anger in his eyes.

"They won't move," he complained.

"They don't trust you yet," the man concluded. "Do not worry. Give it time."

The boy came to the bench every day. He was there when the old man arrived and he stayed until the old man had left. It was thrilling to be at the centre of the performance. He could sense the power of the old man's commands. The rhythm, the precision. His heart leapt as the herons flew to the bench to perch just inches from his grasp.

Occasionally, the man would pass him the packet of fish. And the herons began to trust the boy. They would take the fish he offered, but he could not make them do anything else. They ignored his instructions and he grew frustrated. He was sure he was doing everything right. His gaze, his gestures, his noises were indistinguishable from those of the old man. And yet, the birds eyed him with suspicion.

Eventually, he lost his temper.

"Stupid birds," he shouted and threw a chunk of fish at a heron, then as it flapped out of the way, he began to pelt them all with the contents of the packet, sending the birds swirling high above the trees.

The old man rose to his feet.

"Stop," he thundered. "Stop at once."

The boy had already stopped.

"They're stupid," the boy complained. "They're rude and stupid. And you said they would trust me."

"It seems I was wrong," the old man replied.

The boy fled the park. He rushed across the busy roads. Horns blared, people shouted. He shouted back. He ran up and down until he found the railway bridge, and then he plunged into the darkest, gloomiest depths of his little park.

But it was midday and the boy could not stay in the shadows for long. He came out when the kids arrived to play football. He watched them for a while, then went to the pond, where he sat quietly and squinted at the reeds hoping one revealed itself as a heron. He didn't move until the sun had set and the evening breeze chilled his shoulders.

The next morning, the old man found the boy waiting on the bench as usual. He stared hard at him before taking his seat.

"I did not expect to see you again," he said.

"I didn't mean the herons any harm, I swear," said the boy.

"You will have to prove it to them, not me," the old man informed him. "It will not be easy. You have already shown them who you are."

"I'm going to show them I am like them."

"And what are they like?"

"They are like reeds," the boy explained. "And they can go for hours without moving. So I've decided. I'm going to sit here and I'm not going to move. I'm not going to move until they see they can trust me."

"We shall see what happens."

Herons were already gathering in the trees. The old man opened the white package and began the performance. The boy sat poised and upright and hoped the birds would come to feed. They came, but did not respond when the man summoned them to the bench. They would not come near the boy. The man fed them until the packet was empty and then got up to leave. The boy did not move.

"You can go now," the man told him.

"Give it time. That's what you said."

"I did."

"So I'll stay."

The boy remained on the bench until the man returned in the afternoon to check on him. He brought a sandwich and a flask of tea. But the boy refused to eat. It was a trick, he thought, to get him to move. But the man insisted.

"The herons will understand," he explained. "You saw how they love to eat."

Later, when the shadows stretched across the grass, the old man brought a coat, long and dark, and very much like his own.

"It's time to go home," he said. "There are no herons to witness your endeavour."

"I must prove it to myself," the boy replied.

The old man sighed.

"Then I shall be your witness," said the old man, draping the coat over the boy's shoulders before sitting down by his side.

The boy's body began to ache, his muscles twitched, his guts grumbled. It felt as if his insides wanted to climb out, while his outsides wanted to cave in. He wanted to fidget and squirm. Had the old man not been there, he would surely have given up, but instead he kept upright and did not make a sound.

The old man broke the silence.

"We have company," he said, nodding to the boy's right, where a heron stood on the grass. The boy allowed himself to turn so he could look directly at the bird. He smiled. He thought he recognised the first heron, the one from the reeds by the pond, though they all looked much the same.

"How long has it been there?" he asked.

"For a while now," the old man replied. "You didn't notice?"

"No."

"There's one in the tree also."

The boy glanced up and saw the heron half-concealed by the leaves. A third perched among the lantern-blooms of the horse chestnut behind them.

The old man got to his feet.

"That's enough for today," he said.

With a dramatic flourish and a flick of the fingers, he sent the three herons swirling into the night sky.

The next morning, there was a buzz of excitement at the bench. The boy sat nervously awaiting the old man's arrival. The herons had begun to gather. The old man appeared and without a word handed the boy the packet of fish.

The boy took a deep breath and opened the package. He picked out a small morsel of herring and tossed it onto the path. He selected a bird, fixed it with his gaze, and invited it to eat. The bird flew down and devoured the fish. This was the moment. The boy made the clicking sound and the bird looked at him for instruction. He summoned it to the bench with a smooth, expansive gesture. The bird spread its wings and in a single beat landed on the back of the bench in a pose as serene as a marble statue. The boy smiled. The performance had begun.

Every morning, side by side in their long coats, the old man and the boy gave their performance with the herons. They orchestrated the movement of the birds, conducted it, with precise, elegant gestures, so the tempo flowed and swelled and burst with action. Passers-by would stop to watch. The boy felt their eyes upon him and he liked it. He grew more confident, until one day, bored with their routine, he decided to try a new trick.

Before summoning a bird to the bench, the boy flipped his hand with a sudden, startling motion and the

A BOY IN A PARK

bird made a sudden, startling somersault in response. The crowd gasped and applauded and the boy smiled. He was very pleased with himself.

The old man waited until the end of the performance–when they shared a sandwich and a flask of tea–before he spoke to the boy.

"Do not do that again?" he said sternly.

"Do what?" the boy asked, though he knew exactly what the old man was talking about.

"The herons are not our play things," the man continued. "They are not our puppets."

"But the people liked it."

"Forget about the people. We're here for the herons. No one else. Do you understand?"

The boy nodded.

"It took months, many many months, before the herons would respond to me the way they have for you. For you, it happened in a matter of weeks. You have a gift. Do not abuse it."

Not long after that, the old man announced he would be going away for a few days. He asked the boy if he could trust him to look after the herons while he was gone. The boy said he could. Arrangements had been made for him to collect the off-cuts from the fishmonger, as for the rest, the boy already knew what to do, he said.

The boy did as he'd been asked. He collected the fish, fed the herons, and gave the performance. But it was lonely without the old man by his side and as the days passed and the old man failed to return, the boy began to worry. He waited for him in the morning, looked for him in the crowd. Sometimes he thought he'd glimpsed his tall figure elsewhere in the park, but it was never him. He asked the fishmonger, but the fishmonger knew nothing. He had instructions to prepare the packet of fish until he heard otherwise and that was all.

And then one day, the boy decided the old man would not be coming back. He was dead, or dying, and that was why he had taken the boy under his wing, to prepare him as his replacement. He gulped as he suddenly felt the weight of responsibility that had been passed to him. But the old man had not asked him if he wanted it; he had not even said 'goodbye', and the boy was angry with him.

That day, when he invited the herons to the bench, the boy did not stop at one or two. He didn't stop at three or four or five. He kept calling the herons until all had come down and the bench was full. The last to arrive had nowhere to perch but on the boy's head. It was funny - and the crowd thought so too. The boy could sense their mood. He knew they were desperate to see what would happen next so he delayed, not moving a muscle, sitting poised and upright among the herons, letting their anticipation build, until suddenly, when the time was right, he rose to his feet. The on-lookers gasped as the herons soared in unison, blooming like fireworks in the daylight, rising high above the trees before swooping one by one into the surrounding trees with a satisfying ruffle.

As word spread about the boy's performances, the size of the crowds swelled. People would arrive early to get the best view. The boy was greeted with applause when he arrived and exalted by it at the end. They threw coins by the side of the bench and the boy began to earn a small wage for his labour. He bought himself a trilby, like the old man had worn, and spent the rest on fish for the herons.

The show got bigger and longer and the boy began to wonder why it should be confined to the bench, with the same scenery, the same trees and the same grass every day? Why not move around? He was sure he could get the herons to move. He could lead them wherever he wanted. What was to stop him?

The next performance began at the bench as usual, but from there proceeded across the park, one chunk of fish at a time. The herons sailed alongside the boy, sometimes ahead of him, sometimes behind. The crowd followed, picking up numbers along the way. The boy marched across the road at the end of the lake and led the procession toward the centre of the town.

People came out of offices and shops to witness the peculiar spectacle of a boy in a long coat and trilby leading a surging crowd along the street as herons swooped overhead, from one side to the other, skimming the tops of the buses and trams.

It seemed to the boy the whole town was watching and when he reached the main square, he turned triumphantly to conclude the performance. The crowd gathered around him. He produced the white package with the remaining cuts of fish and looked around for a bird to invite to eat. He spotted one on perched high on lamppost. He fixed it with his gaze and tossed a chunk of fish onto the paving stones.

But the bird ignored the offer and instead of dropping to the boy's feet, it flew away. The boy was taken aback. The crowd started to whisper–he was losing them. He scanned the ledges and rooftops of the square.

It was vast with the grim cathedral at one end, the Guild House at the other, no trees. And not a single heron. Not one. They had disappeared. Blood rushed to the boy's cheeks. Seagulls swooped and squabbled over the fish. The crowd began to disperse.

The boy dropped the package and fled.

He ran in the same direction as the heron and glanced toward the rooftops hoping to catch a glimpse of his birds against the empty blue sky. He knew neither where he was nor where he might be headed. He didn't care. It didn't matter. He kept running and only stopped when he reached the quayside and found he could go no further. Seagulls circled overhead, pigeons scattered on the cobbles, but there was no sign of the herons. He turned and moved along the water's edge, past the barges and yachts and daytripping boats. He broke into a run once more. He reached a small park of iron sculptures, scots pines, and concrete benches and came to sudden, shocking halt.

There, on one of those benches, was the old man in his long, dark coat and trilby. The old man looked up. He seemed tired, hunched, his eyes dark and watery. But he recognised the boy and smiled and the boy rushed to him and buried his head in his side.

"I thought you were dead. I thought you were dead and you weren't coming back."

The boy began to sob.

"But what has happened? Why are you crying?" the old man asked. "What have you done? Tell me."

The boy sat up and wiped his eyes.

"I lost the herons," he confessed. "I led them into town. There was a huge crowd, and then the herons disappeared. I don't know where they went. I didn't even see them go."

"You led them into town?"

"And I lost them. I let you down."

"Well, the herons come and go as they wish. You can't lose them. They're not yours to lose."

"You're not angry with me?"

"Why should I be angry?"

"Because I treated the herons like circus clowns and you told me not to do that."

"I think it would've been better to have not done that. Don't you?"

The boy nodded.

"What should I do now?" he asked.

The old man lifted both arms in a grand gesture of apparent indifference.

"Go home. Go to the park. Stay here. It's all the same," he said. "But if you want to see the herons, you already know what you must do. Collect the fish and present yourself. The herons will find you. Or they won't. Give it time."

The boy thought for a moment.

"I think I'd like to stay here," he said. "The herons will come."

THE CAROUSEL

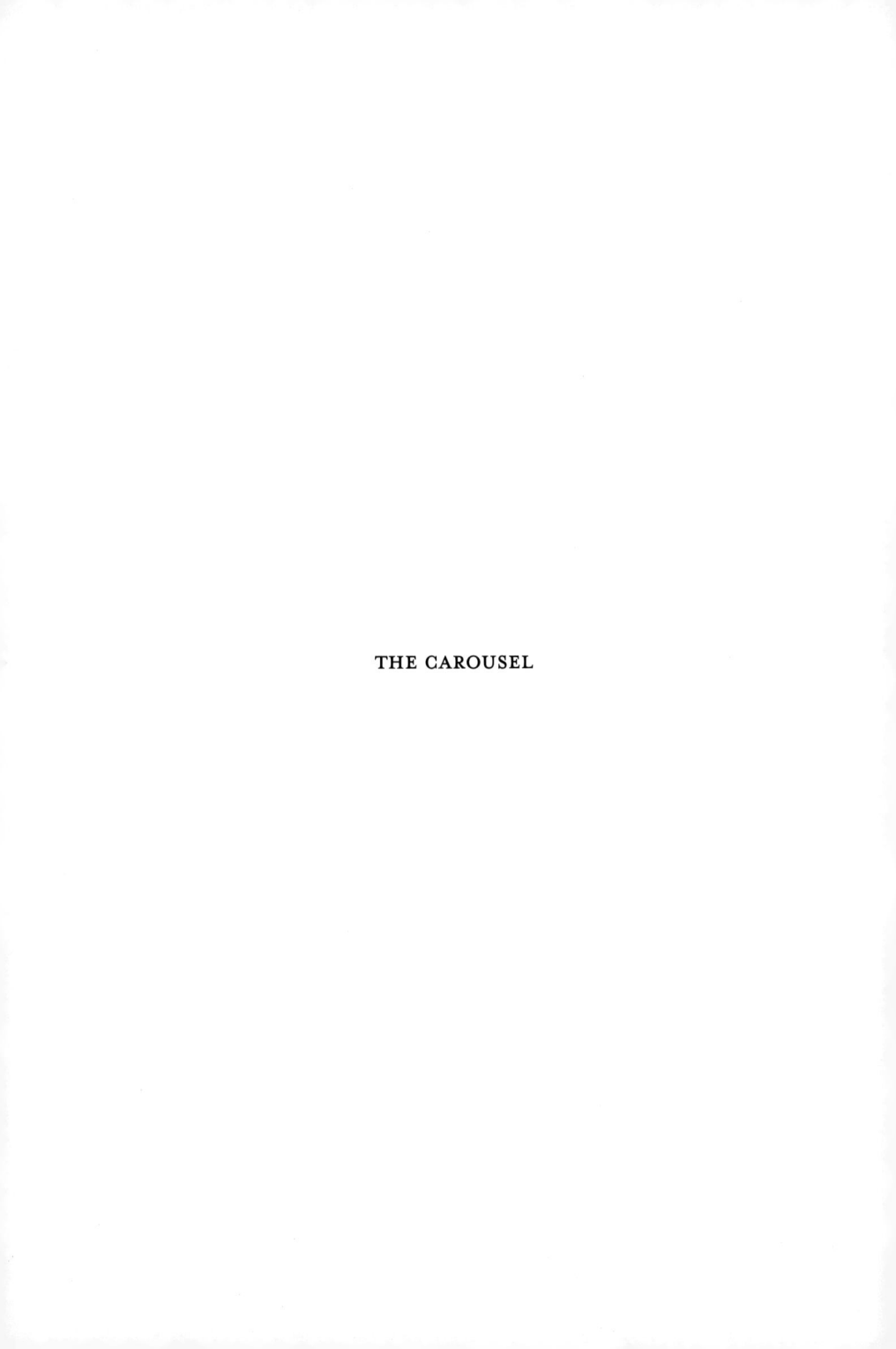

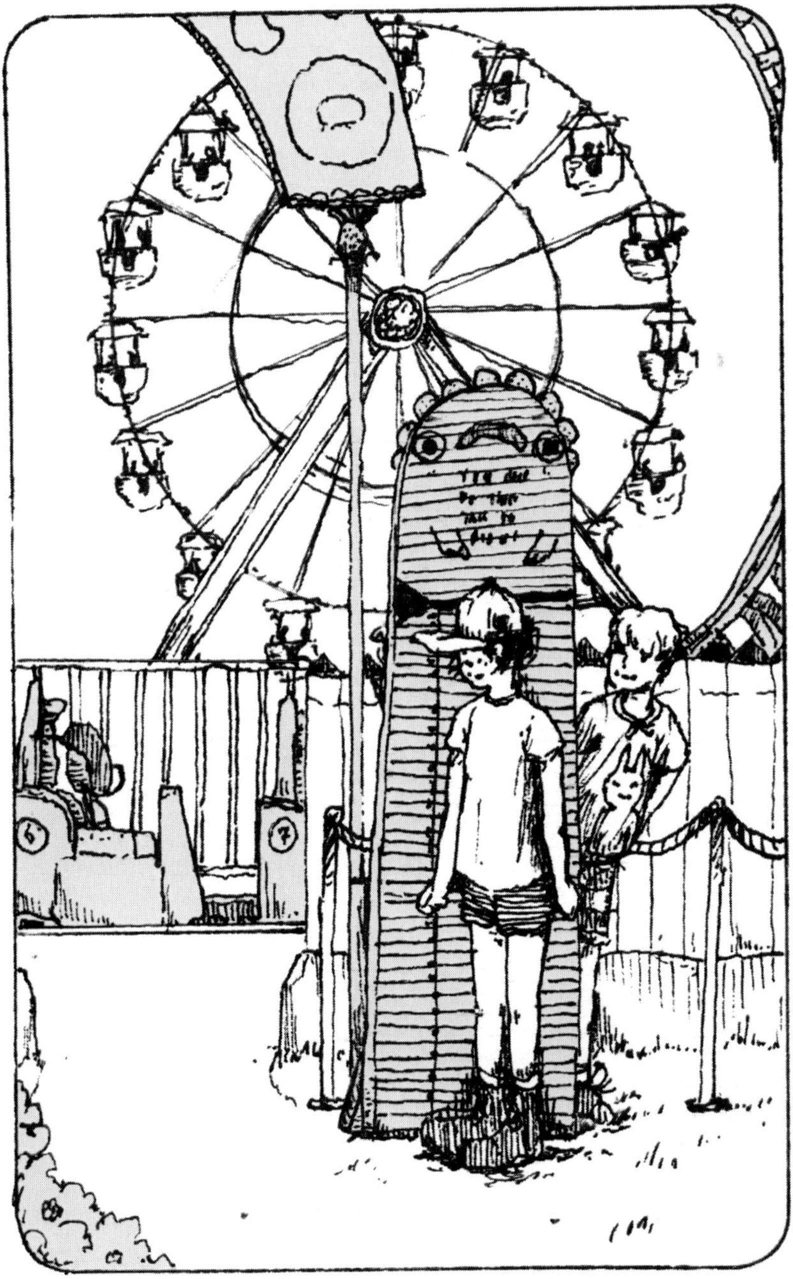
6
7

Once there was a boy who lived in a park.

It was not one of those quiet parks with grass and flowerbeds, lawns and old wooden benches. It was something else entirely. An amusement park, full of noise and excitement, with rollercoasters, slot machines, and cafes selling chips and doughnuts and cola.

And the boy loved it.

There was so much to do, so many different rides. He spent his days going from one to the other, round and round, revelling in the sensations each of them offered. There was the rattling, gasping rush of the rollercoaster, the woozy splash of the flume, the twist of the helter-skelter. And there was his favourite, the carousel.

It was a magnificent carousel, with seats that seemed to float on air. The boy felt as if he were flying and, though the ride merely rotated in a circle, he imagined at any moment he could break away and go anywhere he pleased. He forgot about everything and it was always a shock and a disappointment when the ride slowed and he was brought back to earth.

The boy had to share the rides with the park's many visitors and he was happy to do so. He welcomed the noise, and the smell, and he didn't mind the queues–a queue added to his sense of anticipation–and among the crowds he found he could moved around unnoticed and that was important.

The boy had to take great care not to be recognised by the people who worked at the park, especially those who manned the gates to the rides. They saw him many times a day and to pass unnoticed he would swap T-shirts, don different caps, jackets, and sunglasses–his 'disguises,' he called them. (It was amazing what you could find in lost property or make disappear as you strolled around.) He'd learned how to skim coins from the slot machines and always seem to have enough in his pocket for a hot dog or an ice cream cone.

He was, it has to be said, a bit of rascal and quite pleased with himself, never more so than when he witnessed the protests of the other kids at being told it was time to go. How they stamped and shouted! It wasn't fair. The kids didn't want to go, but they didn't have a choice. Not that the boy felt sorry for them. They merely reminded him of his good fortune. He didn't have anyone to tell him what to do and he knew as long as he was careful he would never have to leave.

Then one day he met the girl.

It was in the queue for the Vertical Drop. The Vertical Drop was the newest ride, the one everyone wanted to go on. The queues were long and there was also a height restriction. When the girl got to the front, she found she wasn't tall enough. Her friends had already made it through and didn't want to give up their place. So the girl waved them on and wandered away feeling very sorry for herself.

The boy had seen this happen many times and it usually made him feel quite smug, but this time, for some reason, he found he wanted to help. And he knew how. He stepped out of the queue and went to his den where he kept his disguises. He brought back a pair of boots.

"These will make you tall enough for the ride," he said to the girl, pressing the boots into her hands.

The girl gave him a puzzled look.

"Try them," he insisted.

"They're too big," she said.

"That's the point," he countered.

The girl tried them on. They were too big.

"I look like a clown," she said.

He'd also brought a baseball cap. She tucked her hair underneath the cap and puckered her lips. She thought she looked silly.

"Try this too," he said. "It's just a disguise. So they won't recognise you. I promise."

And he was right. When they reached the front of the queue again, the ticket collector didn't recognise the girl or the boy and let them both through.

The girl was delighted.

Afterwards, she didn't want to remove her disguise. She clomped around in the big boots and baseball cap, amusing herself, pretending to be a clown, or a boy, or a clown-boy.

"Where did you get this stuff?" she asked.

"It's a secret," the boy replied. "I'll tell you later."

He asked if she wanted to go on another ride and the girl said 'yes' and together they went on every single one. They gasped and swooped on the rollercoaster, they splashed on the flume, and twisted on the helter-skelter. He bought ice cream, big, swirling cones, with chocolate flakes, and they ate as they climbed high on the Ferris wheel. When the gondola paused, they looked out across the sea, mottled by the shadow of the clouds. At the top, they turned and looked inland and the girl tried to spot the outline of the town where she lived, but it was just over the horizon, she said.

The boy kept his favourite, the carousel, till last. But he had forgotten they could not sit together because the seats were only for one. He sat behind so he could watch her and see how much she was enjoying herself. As the ride began, they gently rose and fell like boats on a turning sea. Then the speed increased, the ride lifted, and they began to glide, to fly, as if at any moment they could simply break away and go wherever they wished and do whatever they pleased.

The boy called out to the girl, but she couldn't hear him. He wondered if she felt the same way he did. If she did, he would tell her it didn't need to end. She could stay in the amusement park forever. There was room for two in his den. They could ride together every day. They could find new disguises. They could eat together. It would be so much fun.

Just then, she tossed her head back and the baseball cap caught the rushing air. The boy reached for it, but it was gone too quickly, spiralling down to the roof of the arcades. The ride too came to an end more quickly than the boy had wanted. He wanted to go again straight away, but the girl wasn't sure.

"My hair's a mess," she said.

"Wait there, I'll get you another cap," the boy said, and he dashed off to fetch one.

When the boy returned, the girl had moved away. He found her chatting and laughing with her friends. If felt as if the door had closed. He was going to ask her if she wanted to come and stay with him, but he couldn't say anything in front of her friends. He couldn't let anyone else know he lived in the park. It was a secret.

"I need to ask you something," he said.

Her friends smirked.

"I have to go home now," the girl replied.

The boy lost his nerve.

"I got you another cap," he said, handing her another cap.

"I've got your boots," the girl replied.

The girl had taken off the boots and tied them together by the laces. The boy didn't want to take them. He knew if he took them it meant it was over, she was going home.

"We haven't been on the dodgems yet," he declared with forced excitement. "Or the arcades. I've got so much else to show you."

"Maybe tomorrow," the girl replied.

"Tomorrow. Okay," said the boy and he began to think that would be a good idea. They would have more time tomorrow. They could do all the rides again and all the other things and she would have such a good time that when he asked her to stay she would say 'yes' without hesitation.

The girl squeezed his arm and whispered, "thank you," then she began to walk away.

"I'll see you tomorrow," the boy called out.

"See you tomorrow," she replied.

But they didn't see each other the next day. The girl didn't come back. The weather was good and her family went to the beach instead. She didn't have a choice. The day after that, their holiday was over. They packed up and went back to the city.

The boy hung around near the entrance waiting for the girl. He didn't go on any rides. He didn't want to risk missing her in the crowds. One of the staff asked if he was lost and he had to hurry back to his den to find a new disguise.

At the end of the day, he gave up. He went to the Ferris wheel. When he reached the top, he tried to spot the town where she said she lived, but it still was just over the horizon.

He waited again the next day, but on the third he returned to his amusements. The rattling gasp of the rollercoaster, the woozy splash of the flume, the twist of the helter-skelter, the plunging terror of the Vertical Drop and, best of all, the carousel, the whirling, soaring freedom of the carousel, which made him feel he could break away at any moment and go wherever he wished and do whatever he pleased.

THE LITTLE GHOST

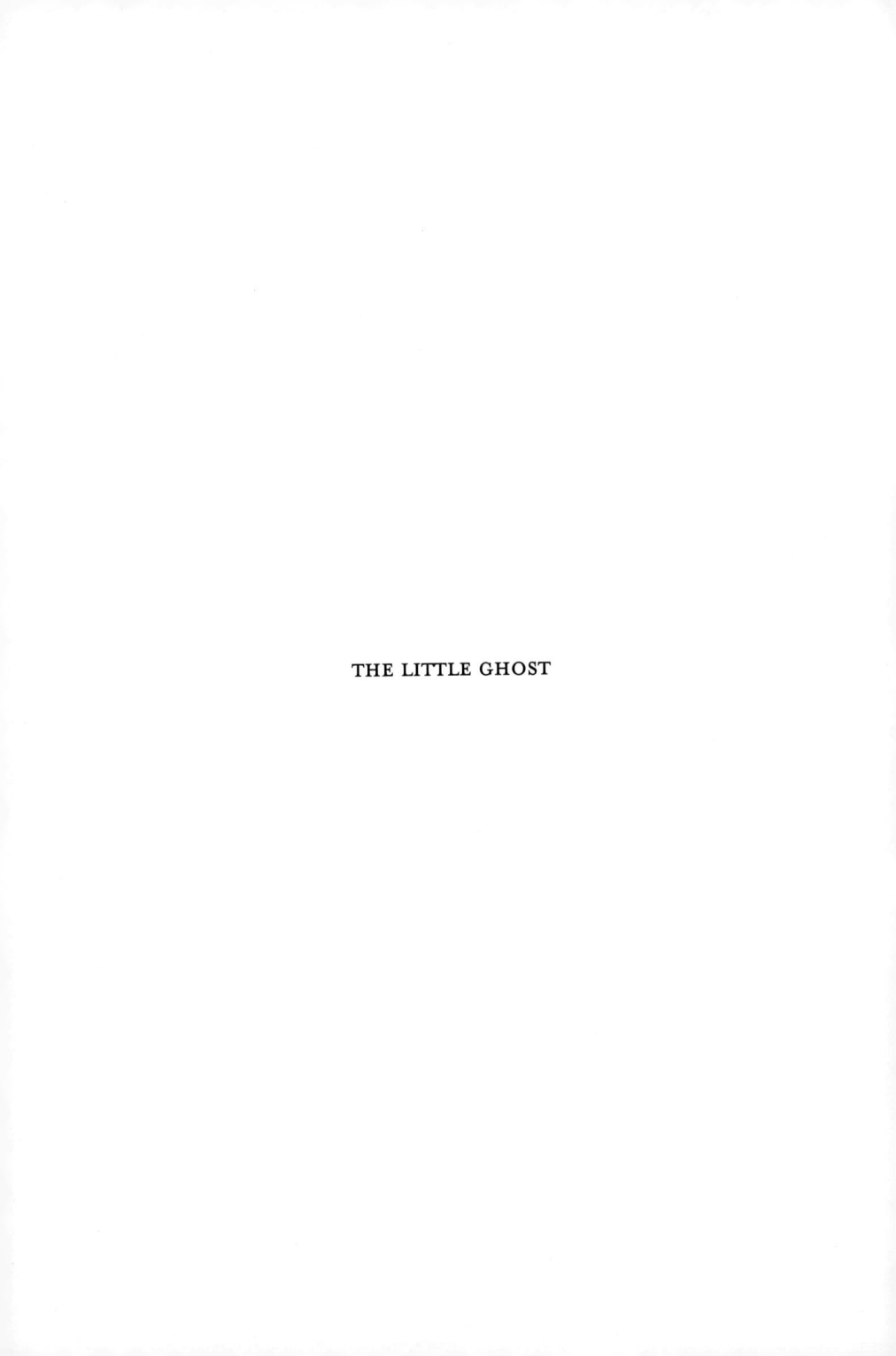

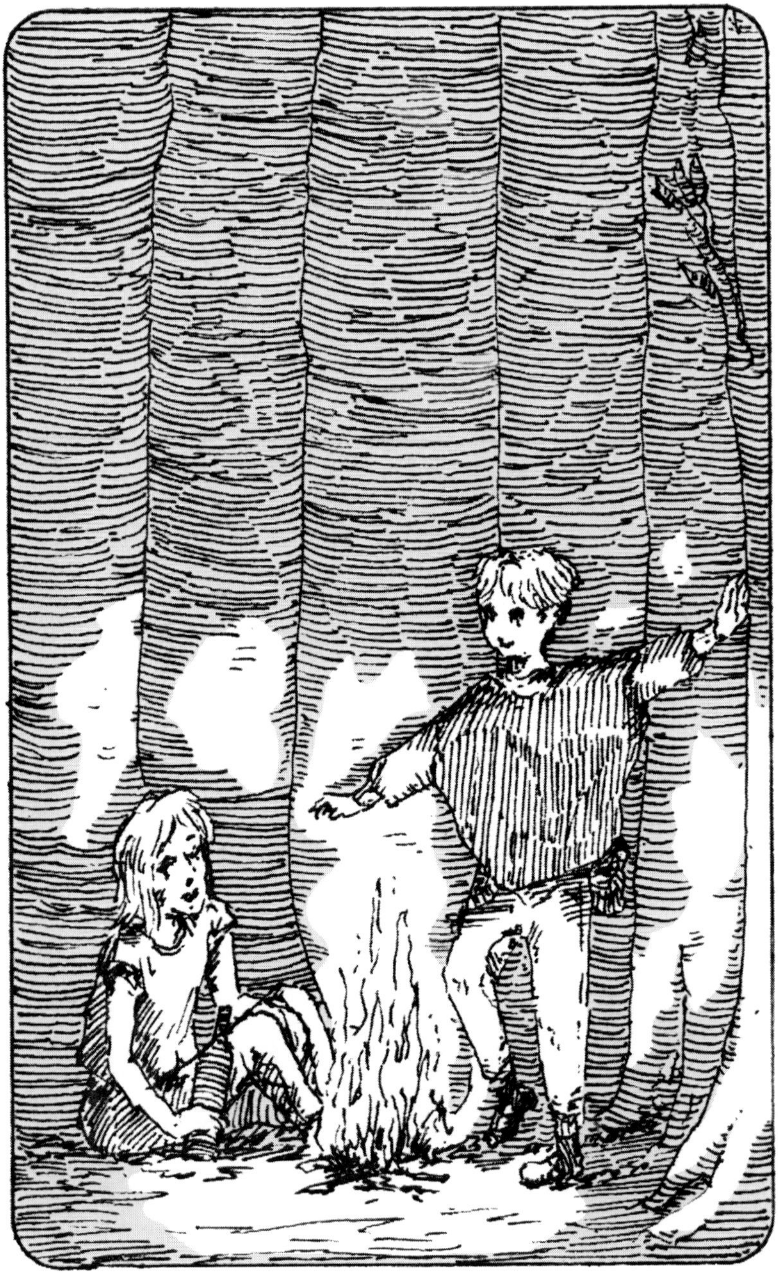

Once there was a boy who lived in a park.

In fact, he lived just outside the park in a derelict shed at the bottom of an old railway embankment. It was a strange place to live, dark and lonely and damp, but then the boy wasn't really living, not in the way you or I would understand. He had been dead for months, but had not yet realised. This was not a pleasant condition.

The boy had forgotten who he was and where he lived and no one would help him. People either ignored him or shrank away. He wandered the streets bewildered and ashamed. But he kept returning to the shed at the bottom of the railway embankment where he felt secure and eventually he settled there.

He started to make a new life for himself with new routines. He would visit the park every day. He would climb the slope, huddle by the fence, and listen to the sounds of ordinary life passing by. He found if he simply closed his eyes and listened he could imagine himself part of the world again, among the rattle of buggies and prams on the tarmac paths, the wail of toddlers stumbling in the playground, the barking of dogs.

Later, around dusk, he would sneak into the yards of the nearby houses and hunker down beneath the windows to listen to what went on inside. He heard the bubbling of saucepans, the ping of microwaves, and kids called to eat, over and over. And he would tune in to the curious, stilted melody of questions and complaints, requests and refusals that passes between people when they gather for a meal. And he could imagine himself there at the table with them.

But it was not enough.

One night, he gave in to temptation and pressed his face against the glass of the window. It was a mistake. When he saw the family together, he was reminded of what he'd lost and let out a long, keening moan. He gave himself away. There were startled gasps and cries; somebody came to the door, and the boy bolted like a frightened animal. He crashed over the fence, rolled into the alleyway, and scrambled down the embankment to the safety of the little shed. There he fell on the concrete floor panting and sobbing until had nothing left.

Later, he woke to the sound of movement outside the shed. He sat up and listened. It was a slow, shuffling noise, something pushing through the undergrowth. A large animal, he thought, a badger or a fox. It seemed to circle the shed and move off and he went back to sleep.

In the morning, he climbed the embankment and huddled against the fence as usual, but he dared not close his eyes. He felt exposed. He feared people would be looking for him because of his intrusion. He feared they would find him and drive him away from what little he had left in the word. After less than an hour, he withdrew quietly to the shed.

That night, he woke to the same slow, shuffling

noises. He told himself there was nothing to worry about. It was just an animal. But then came a sudden bang on the wall, hard and spiteful. The boy sat up. His heart beat against his ribs. Someone was out there. They had found him. Another blow, harder than the first, struck the opposite wall. The boy shrank into the corner and braced for the worse. The entire building began to shake. The corrugated roof rattled against the old wooden planks that kept it upright. It was going to fall. It was going to fall on his head.

Beyond the park and the old railway embankment lay a confusing expanse of common land, a mess of woods, rough, greasy meadows, and abandoned quarries, half-managed, half-neglected. It was into these the boy set out the next day. The roof had not fallen on his head, the walls had not collapsed upon him, nor had anyone attempted to enter his makeshift home. But he had been discovered, he was sure of that. They would come for him; it was just a matter of time.

Shortly after he set out, he sensed he was being followed. He looked around. There was no sign of anyone or anything. It was just a feeling, a finger, hard and bony, poking into his ribs. He changed direction, doubled back, trying to shake the feeling, but the feeling stayed with him.

It began to rain, a light drizzle that smeared the open spaces and clung to the trees. He found a black bin bag and put his head through it to make a waterproof tunic. But the rain hardened and he looked instead for shelter. He crawled beneath a thicket of hawthorn, but water trickled through the plaited branches. He pushed forward and on the other side he discovered an abandoned camp. A thick plastic sheet, a tarpaulin, hung across two trees and a rough-hewn pole. The tarp was dark and heavy and loomed over him like a bird of prey. The ground beneath the tarp was dry. A sleeping bag lay crumpled beside the remains of a small campfire. He poked the ashes with a stick. It was cold. With the rain beating on the canopy, he lay down and let himself fall asleep.

When the boy opened his eyes, the rain had stopped. A silvery light filtered through the trees beyond the tarp. Someone was sitting on a tree stump on the other side of the campfire. An older lad with long, greasy hair, bony shoulders, and a prominent broken tooth.

"Mornin'," said the lad.

The boy tried to scrambled to his feet.

"Where are you going now?" the lad asked.

The boy stopped. It had been so long since someone spoke to him like that. Calm and direct. He was confused. And pleased.

"So tell me, d'you make a habit of poking around other people's homes?" the lad continued.

"Is this your home?" the boy asked.

"Well, it's not yours, is it?"

The boy thought of his shed. He'd like to have remained there.

"It was raining," he explained.

"Yeah, it was foul, wasn't it? No weather to be out and about."

The strange lad started to undo the tarp.

"You must be thirsty," he said.

"I suppose," the boy replied.

"Here you go then."

The strange lad released the tarp and a pool of water that had collected on the top spilled over the boy.

"Hey," the boy protested.

The strange lad doubled with laughter.

"Lucky you're wearing a bin bag," he gasped, but suddenly became serious again. He handed the boy a towel and watched him as he dried himself.

"Are you gonna help with this or not?" he asked as he returned to the tarpaulin.

The boy obliged. He could not help himself. The strange lad intimidated him and flattered him at the same time. They folded the tarpaulin, laid it on the ground, rolled it up, and then the strange lad tied it in place.

"Where's your stuff?" he asked as he picked up his backpack.

"I don't have anything," the boy replied.

"That's a bit odd, don't you think?"

The boy hadn't thought about it, but it was a bit odd, he agreed.

"You take this then," the strange lad said, dropping the backpack in front of the boy. Then he heaved the tarp onto his shoulder and strode off.

"Come on," he called from the edge of the trees.

The boy picked up the backpack and bending under its weight trudged towards him.

"Where are we going?" he asked.

"Not far," the strange lad replied. "Gotta keep moving. Otherwise, they'll get you. In't that right?"

The boy followed the strange lad with broken tooth through the scrubby common land. He kept

A BOY IN A PARK

falling behind, under the weight of the backpack, but the strange lad would stop frequently and head off in a different direction as if he were looking for something. Eventually he set the tarp down and raised his finger to silence the boy.

"Watch this," he whispered, then he crept forward, crumbled a biscuit onto the trunk of a fallen tree, and retreated. He pulled a catapult and a couple of stones from his pocket. The squirrel came down for the biscuit. The boy winced as the stone hit the squirrel smack on the head and knocked it off the trunk. The strange lad whooped in triumph.

"Go get it," he ordered.

The boy found the squirrel behind the trunk. Its head oozed blood, but it wasn't dead, not quite, the body twitching, its eyes glassy and wide. He didn't want to touch the poor creature. The strange lad appeared at his side.

"What's the matter? Haven't you seen a dead thing before?"

"It's not dead," the boy explained.

The strange lad gave the boy a pointed look before grabbing the squirrel by the tail and dashing its brains on the tree trunk.

"I think it's dead now, don't you?" he said with a grin. "Now go collect wood for the fire. Lots of it. We're going to have a feast tonight."

The boy went to collect wood. He worked until he had an armful and brought it back to the camp. The strange lad sent him off for more. He continued like this until he'd gathered enough wood for a small bonfire. At this point, the strange lad was not around to congratulate him or set him to another task. The camp was empty. The tarp had been hung, while large, flat stones had been arranged in a circle for the fire. The boy rested against a tree trunk and thought how lucky he'd been to find a new friend and a new place in the world.

A hard, bony finger poked the boy awake.

"You're a sleepy one, int'ya?"

The strange lad leant over him, his broken tooth disfiguring his broad grin.

"Time to get your hands dirty," he continued, then led the boy to the fire. "Watch carefully."

Half-a-dozen squirrel carcasses were piled by his side. He took one and cut off the head. The boy was horrified.

"It's gotta be done," the strange lad explained, as he pulled the skin from the carcass, sliced open the belly, and reached inside to claw out the guts and internal organs, which he slapped down on the edge of the fireplace with relish.

"Your turn," he said, offering the boy the knife.

The boy shook his head.

"I'm not hungry," he said.

"Is that so? When was the last time you ate?"

The boy didn't have an answer to this question. He'd eaten, of course he had, but he couldn't remember the last time.

"Yesterday," he lied.

"Yeah? What did you eat?"

"Bread. Bread and ice cream," the boy replied.

"Bread and ice cream?"

The strange lad roared with derision, then suddenly got serious.

"Get lost," he spat. "Go on. Get lost."

The boy didn't move.

A BOY IN A PARK

"Go on."

The boy began to shuffle away. He was almost in tears. He didn't understand what was going on.

"Ah, come back, come back," the strange lad called, softening his tone.

The boy returned and let the strange lad put his arm around him to console him. But the strange lad's grip tightened and he pressed two fingers onto the boy's forehead, leaving a smear of blood and squirrel innards. The boy winced as if the gore had burned him.

"There," he said. "That's brought you down to earth. We're going to be eating squirrel tonight so you'd better get to it."

The boy did as he was told. He skinned and gutted the remaining squirrels, while the strange lad began to work on the fire. The damp kindling would not light and sent up only a wispy plume of smoke. It was almost dark by the time flames began to rise through the larger sticks. Smoke swirled and billowed beneath the shelter of the tarpaulin.

The boy suddenly became anxious.

"Won't somebody see us?" he asked.

"Like who?" the strange lad retorted.

"You said somebody was after you. That's what you said."

"I did? Oh, you mean the locals," the strange lad replied. "They don't come out at night. They're cowards. All tucked up in front of the TV."

"I think they came after me last night," the boy replied.

"Yeah? Did you see them?"

"No, but–"

"But did they have flash lights? You'd have seen those."

The boy fell silent. He hadn't seen flashlights. The damp wood hissed.

"Does anything else come out at night?" he asked eventually.

"Well, there's animals, o'course. Badgers, foxes, owls, and such. And ghosts. Coulda been ghosts."

"Ghosts," said the boy quietly, as if to himself.

"Have you seen a ghost?"

"Oh yeah, sure."

"What are they like?"

"Well, they aren't wispy and see-through like you think. They look like normal people, like you or me, only they make you feel weird, give you weird sensations, like your skin crawls or you feel icy cold inside, that kind of thing."

"Are they nasty?"

"You mean violent? Can be. It depends. They get possessive and attach themselves to things and places, that's why you have to keep moving."

"Are they coming after you?"

"Ha, no! It's me who's coming after them. I'm a ghost hunter, see."

Flashing the boy another grin, he picked up a squirrel carcass, stuck a sharpened stick right through it, and laid it over the fire.

The night closed in. The boy and the strange lad stared into the fire. It sizzled and flared as fat dropped from the roasting squirrels. The boy imagined himself laid on the flames like the poor animals, his skin melting away.

"Is it hard to get rid of ghosts?" he asked.

"Thing about ghosts, they don't know they're

dead," the strange lad explained. "Soon as they do, they're gone, poof, like smoke. Easy. Getting 'em there's the hard part."

"How could they not know?" the boy puzzled.

"Beats me."

The strange lad rummaged around in his backpack and pulled out a bottle of red wine.

"Been saving it," he said, before taking a long swig. Then he held it out for the boy. "You've had wine before, haven't you?"

The boy nodded, but it wasn't true.

"Get it down you," the strange lad insisted.

By the time the squirrels were roasted and ready to eat, the two of them were drunk. They gnawed on the charred flesh, crunching on bone and gristle, pulling faces and burping.

The boy began to feel strange, his head spinning while his body grew heavy, as if the food were weighing him down. He got to his feet and stood there for a moment, not knowing what he had intended to do. Then he started to dance. But he didn't know how to dance. He circled the fire, bobbing up and down, kicking his legs to the side, one after the other, and thrusting his arms into the air.

The strange lad thought it was hilarious.

"What are you doing?" he shouted. "You're a madman."

"I'm doing a dance," the boy replied. "To ward off the ghosts."

Then began to chant: "Waah-oooh, way-oooh. Waah-oooh, way-oooh."

The dance got faster, and wilder, with help from the strange lad who started pounding the stone fireplace like a drum. The boy's head whirled and spun as if it were about to come loose from his shoulders and soar into the night sky. And then he stumbled, stopped, swayed. The trees, the tarp, the fire continued to revolve around him. He felt sick. He lurched into the darkness, then turned back to the campfire where he dropped on all fours and vomited a thin, reddish gruel flecked with gobbets of half-digested squirrel flesh.

At dawn, the rain started to fall again, drumming gently on the tarpaulin and tapping on the boy's feet, which stuck out from beneath the canopy. The boy groaned. His head throbbed, his throat was sore, this was coldest time of the morning. He sat up. The strange lad sprawled half-in, half-out of his greasy sleeping bag, a squirrel bone stuck in his hair, a rough, low-pitched snore rolling from an open mouth.

The boy had thought the camp might be his new home, but now he wasn't so sure. He longed for his quiet little shed in the depths of the old railway embankment. Most of all, he wanted to visit the park and listen to the reassuring sounds of prams and dogs and toddlers. He decided to leave. But the moment he got to his feet, he felt the strange lad's hand gripping his ankle.

"You going somewhere?"

"To get something to drink," the boy lied.

"If you're thirsty, all you need to do is open your mouth," the strange lad replied and he demonstrated by sticking his head from under the canopy and letting the rain hit his face.

"Actually I want to go home," the boy replied.

The strange lad released the boy's ankle.

"Course you do," he said with surprising tenderness.

The boy hesitated. He could never tell when the strange lad was serious.

"Go on. Go Back to your little shed," the strange lad urged.

The boy found his way home, though it took him most of the morning. When he got there, he found nothing but a pile of debris: a sheet of corrugated iron, rotten wooden planks, bricks. His shed had been demolished. He sank to his knees and stretched his arms over the pile of debris, embracing it as if it were a coffin or a corpse. He began to sob. It was his fault, he told himself. He should have been there. He should never have left. But if the ghosts returned, he resolved to challenge them. He would vanquish them.

He sat by the pile of debris and waited. Flies buzzed around him, small birds fussed in the undergrowth. Around dusk, as the light began to thicken, he got the feeling someone was watching him. That same awkward sensation, but the hard, bony finger was pressing him square in his chest this time.

It was them. They were near.

The boy stood up. Summoning every ounce of his courage, he shouted into the shadows.

"Come on, show yourselves. Show yourselves. I know you're there."

The strange lad with the broken tooth pushed through the undergrowth toward the boy.

"Just me," he grinned.

The boy frowned. The strange lad's smile made him nervous.

"Are you the ghost?" he asked.

The strange lad laughed and changed the subject.

THE LITTLE GHOST

"We could make a fire with that," he said, nodding at the pile of debris.

He set his pack down and began to sort the wood from the brick.

"Why did you choose this place?" he asked without looking up. "I mean, did you just find it by accident? Did you maybe live nearby? Or is this where you died? Am I gonna find your body if I dig too deep down here?"

"I'm not dead."

"No? Okay."

"This was my shed. Ghosts destroyed. Not me."

"Oh, it was me what destroyed it. The night you went wandering off onto the Common. Didn't take long. Reckon, it wanted to go."

The boy gaped at the strange lad, his greasy hair and gnarly, bony shoulders. He could hardly believe what he was saying. He could not comprehend such casual destruction.

"We're going to need some kindling. Strip that birch tree over there, will ya?"

The strange lad came in close as he handed the boy his knife, looking him in the eye, daring him to use it against him. But the boy did as he was told. He went to the undernourished birch sapling and stripped it of its branches.

The strange lad built the fire circle from the brick and used the corrugated iron as a windbreak. The boy brought the kindling and sat down beside him as he put the spark to it.

"I'm not dead. Honestly," the boy insisted.

"Where are your mum and dad?"

"At home."

"And where's that?"

"I've forgotten."
"How long have you been here?"
"Not long."
"But how long? A week, a month, a year, what?"
"I don't know."
"You don't know much."
"I know I'm not dead."
"You're hanging on in there, aren't you? I like that. I do. You're hanging on in, but there's not much left to hold, is there, eh?"

"Shut up," the boy burst out fiercely. "Shut up. Shut up. Shut up."

The fire caught hold. Small peaks of fine, yellow flame licked the wooden planks, which began to squeal with the damp. A thin plume of smoke curled upwards.

"You got anything to eat? I'm starving," the strange lad asked.

"I'm hungry too," the boy replied, his face brightening. "See, I can't be a ghost, can I? Ghosts can't get hungry, can they?"

"Some can," the strange lad explained with a sigh. "Some have a constant hunger they can't never satisfy, some even eat flesh, some are angry all the time, others sad. But I'll tell you something, they're all lonely, they've all got this insatiable longing. All of them. You've got it too. That's right, innit?"

The boy said nothing.

"How about you do that dance again? The one to ward off ghosts?" the strange lad asked. "It'll take your mind off it."

The boy shook his head.

"No?" the strange lad stood. "Let's see if I can remember how it's done."

The strange lad began to dance. He circled the fire, bobbing up and down, kicking his legs to the side, one after the other, thrusting his arms into the air. The smoke swirled around him. He started to chant: "Waah-oooh, way-oooh. Waah-oooh, way-oooh."

The dance got faster, and wilder, and noisier. And then he stopped, abruptly. The world spun beyond him for a moment. Smoke hung in the air.

The boy had gone.

The strange lad sat by the fire and stared into the flames and felt that loneliness, that insatiable longing, take hold of him once more.

THE LOVELY RED BICYCLE
for Alessandra

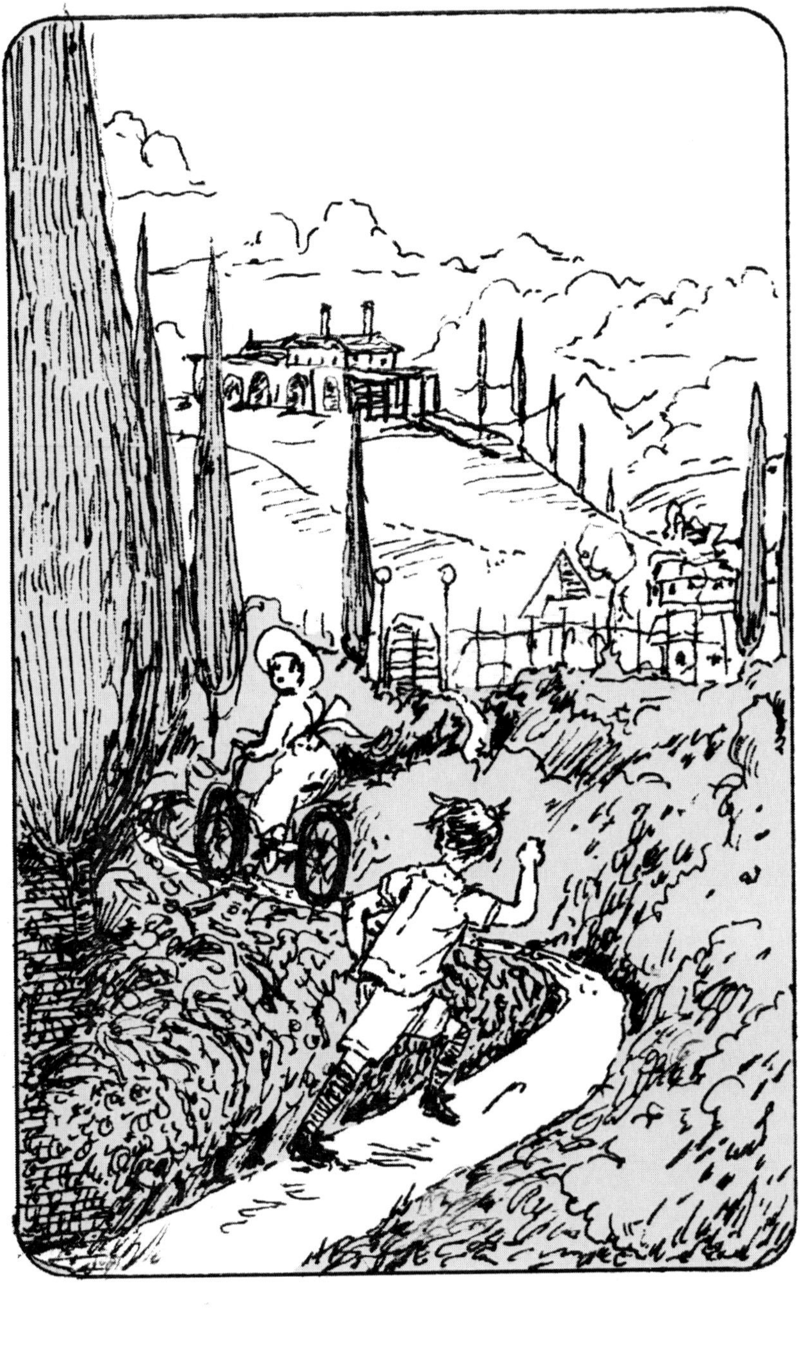

Once there was a boy who lived in a park.

It was a small, dusty park in a quiet corner of the town. Life there was hard, but simple. In winter, the boy curled up with a blanket in the hollow of a bush, while in summer he stretched beneath one of the benches. He lived untroubled until one bright morning a girl pulled up in front of his bench on a lovely red bicycle.

"Do you like my bicycle?" she asked.

The boy looked at the bicycle. It was brand new and the red paintwork shone in the sunshine.

"It looks fast," the boy replied.

"You can have it if you want," she said.

"Really?"

"Yes," the girl replied. "But you'll have to catch me first."

And with that, the girl rode away.

The boy rubbed his eyes. He couldn't quite believe what the girl had said. Would she really give her bicycle to him? He might as well find out. She waited for him further down the path.

"Well," she called. "Do you want it or don't you?"

A BOY IN A PARK

And so the chase began.

Round and round the park, they went, the boy and the girl. The boy was quick on his feet, but the girl had the advantage. The girl had the bicycle. The boy only came close when the girl allowed it and she would squeal with fear and delight as she evaded him just in time.

"Almost got you," the boy would cry, and the chase would go on.

Sometimes the boy would cheat. He would take shortcuts across the grass or hide behind a tree to ambush the girl. But it was no use. The girl saw through his tricks and would play along just to encourage him. She gasped with surprise, but always managed to change direction and speed away at the right moment.

And then one day the boy made up his mind to catch the girl. He would give it everything. It was time. When he next came within reach, he threw himself full-length, arms outstretched, toward the girl. The girl shrieked and wobbled and fell from the bike. This was his chance, but he had landed with a bump face down in the dirt and by the time he picked himself up and wiped the dust from his eyes, the girl was standing by her bicycle brushing herself down too. Her knee grazed.

"You've spoiled everything," she declared, glaring at him, and then she turned and rode from the park.

The next day, the boy waited anxiously for the girl to appear, but she did not come. He paced around the park, chiding himself for the terrible mistake he'd made. He had been reckless and impulsive and had hurt the girl, spoiled their game and would never ever ride the lovely red bicycle.

The girl did not return the following day either, nor the day after that, and the boy realised he had to return to his old routine. Better to live without the excitement and emotions and the hope, he decided. But at that very moment, he heard a familiar voice.

"Hello," said the girl. "Did you miss me?"

"No," the boy lied, but he had missed her more than anything, more than parents, more than a home.

"Are you angry with me?" the girl asked–she could tell he was lying.

"No," the boy replied.

"Because I'm the one who should be angry," she explained. "You were silly and knocked me over. You really shouldn't have done that."

"Sorry," said the boy.

"Yes, and I was all ready to invite you to come and play at my house."

"You were?" said the boy.

"Yes. It's a big house up there on top of the hill."

The girl pointed in the direction of her house, but she needn't have done. The boy had heard about the big house on the hill. If you climbed a tree, which he often did, you could see it high above the rooftops of the old town. It shimmered in the sunshine or glowered in the grey rain. The boy had wondered what life was like up there. How beautiful it must be!

"But do you really live up there?" the boy gasped.

"Where else would I live?" the girl replied.

"Do you think I could come and stay with you one day?" the boy asked.

"Yes, of course. It's a big house and there's plenty of room," she replied. "But you'll have to catch me first."

And with that, the girl rode away.

The boy rubbed his eyes. He couldn't quite believe what the girl had said. Would she really let him come to stay in the big house on the hill?

She was waiting for him further down the path.

"Well?" she called. "Do you want it or don't you?"

And so the chase began again.

Round and round the park, they went, the boy and the girl. The boy was quick on his feet, but the girl had the advantage. The girl had the bicycle. The boy only came close when the girl allowed it and she would squeal with fear and delight as she evaded him just in time.

There were other homeless orphans who lived in and around the dusty little park. They were the boy's friends, most of them, and they watched him chase the girl round and around, day after day. They would shout encouragement when he got close and jeer him when she got away, which she always did. It was splendid entertainment, they thought, though they did not understand the boy's obsession. They doubted the girl would ever give him her lovely red bicycle and they certainly did not believe she would invite him to stay at big house on the hill. It was ridiculous and impossible, they said, and they warned him not to take it so seriously. But he assured them he would get there in the end.

"Just you watch."

As the days and months and years went by, the orphans moved on with their lives. They found new homes and new parents. They found jobs, fell in love, and had children of their own. The boy did not notice them leave. He didn't care. His mind was fixed on the chase. And when others took their place he told them all about the girl's promises, her lovely red bicycle and her invitation to the big house on the hill. He would get there in the end, he assured them.

"Just you watch."

One day, as he sped across the grass to catch the girl, he ran straight into an old man. He hit him so hard the old man fell to the ground. The boy stopped to help him up.

"You need to look where you're going," said the man, checking his glasses for damage.

"Sorry," said the boy, with one eye on the little girl who had paused to wait for him.

When the man put his glasses back his expression suddenly changed.

"It's you!" he exclaimed. "I was hoping I'd see you here."

The boy squinted at the man. He'd never seen him before.

"When I heard they were going to turn our dusty little park into a big roundabout, I had to come and see it again one last time. Have you seen any of the others?"

"Others?"

"All the other waifs and strays who used to live around here."

The boy glanced around the little park. There had been other children. He remembered them: their voices, cheering him, shouting at him, but none of them were there now.

"I haven't seen anyone. Not for a long time," the boy replied.

The man nodded.

"You must have been busy," he said.

The boy nodded. It was true, he thought. He had been very busy.

"I suppose we all have," the man continued, and he began to tell the boy about his life: how he'd gone to live with a shopkeeper in the suburbs, how he'd studied quite hard and got a steady job, how his new parents had died, one after the other, and he'd been very sad, but his wife had been there to comfort him and there was his lovely daughter too, who was almost as old as that little girl with the red bicycle, the one the boy used to chase around.

"Whatever became of her?" the man asked.

The boy's head was spinning. The man was talking as if years had passed, as if the little girl had grown up, as if she were an adult. But that didn't make sense. The boy had been chasing the girl all morning and she was as youthful and lovely as she'd ever been.

"She was here a moment ago," said the boy with concern as he looked around and saw the girl was no longer waiting for him on the other side of the lawn. "She must have gone home."

"I guess you never did catch her," the man laughed as if he thought he'd made a joke.

The boy glared at him.

"But I will," the boy replied. "One of these days. Just you watch."

The man's stupid joke had stung the boy and he was now more determined than ever to catch the girl. It was time she made good on that invitation, he thought, and he decided to go directly to the house on the hill. They could continue their games up there. He crossed the road and left the park behind.

But he didn't know the way. All he knew was the house was on top of the hill above the old town. So he set off through the cobbled streets, always opting for the alleyway or street that led him upwards. Beyond the old town, he found a road that continued up the hill in smooth, tarmacked hairpins. Here the houses were set back behind whitewashed walls and high fences. He ignored them. His goal was the highest and biggest house of all, the one on top of the hill.

But when he got there, he found the gate would not open.

"Hello," he called. "It's me. Are you there?"

The boy gripped the bars of the gate and shook them until–it seemed–the intercom crackled. A hard, aggressive voice issued from the little box. The voice asked what he wanted. He wanted to see his friend, he said. He'd been invited. But the voice told him they weren't expecting any visitors that day. The boy hesitated. It was true. They weren't expecting him. He hadn't been invited. Not yet. He would only be invited if he caught the girl.

"I'll wait," the boy said, and he retreated to the other side of the road.

From there, he could look down over the rooftops of the old town. It seemed so small, squeezed on either side by the suburbs and factories that filled the valley. Beyond that, a highway busy with traffic split the parched countryside. 'What were they doing?' he wondered. 'Where were they all going?'

After a while, the boy went home.

A BOY IN A PARK

The little park seemed very small and dirty and it would soon be covered in cement and tarmac and made into a roundabout for cars and buses and motorbikes. He slumped on his bench—though it wasn't really his bench, it was just a bench under which he slept. He'd slept there for as long as he could remember and he'd done nothing but chase the girl for as long as he could remember. There was nothing else.

At that moment, he heard a familiar voice. He hardly dared look up, but he when he did he saw the girl standing beside the lovely red bicycle, smiling, as if nothing had ever happened.

"Are you crying?" she asked.

"No," the boy replied, wiping his cheeks, which to his surprise were wet.

"Good," said the girl. "Because you ought to be happy."

"Why?" the boy asked.

"Well, I heard they were turning the park into a roundabout so I've decided it's time you came and lived with me instead."

"Really?" said the boy. "In the big house on the hill?"

"Where else?" the girl replied.

"Thank you," the boy sighed.

"But you'll have to catch me first."

And with that, the girl rode away.

But this time she didn't have to wait further down the path. The boy was already on his feet and she was already furiously pedalling away.

THE TOMB

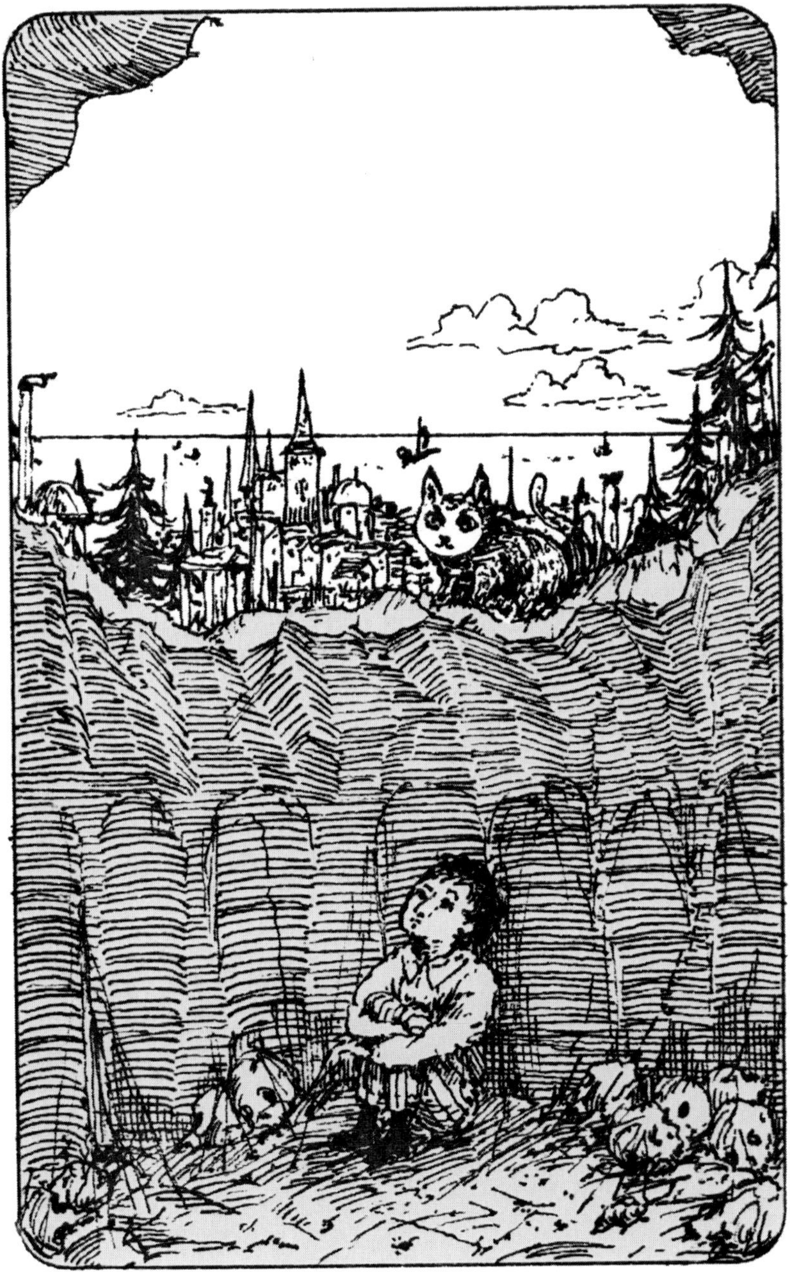

Once there was a boy who lived in a park.

It was the most beautiful park in a city renowned for beautiful parks. Towering pines stood guard over ancient ruins, dusty paths looped through arcades of honeysuckle and jasmine, while a gentle slope of sunbaked grass, shaded by evergreen oaks, opened views across spires and domes and slanting terracotta rooftops.

Every day, visitors arrived by the coach-load to swoon and sigh at its eternal splendour. But the boy was unmoved. The park was his home. He could see the view every day. It was normal. It was boring. And besides, he cared about one thing and one thing only: daydreaming.

He loved to daydream and he was very good at it. He'd started with idle fantasies, like getting locked in an ice-cream parlour and not leaving until he'd sampled every flavour, or playing a monster emerging from the slime of the river to frighten the visitors with ghoulish howls of pain. But he'd soon discovered more complex and intriguing possibilities and of these the most complex and intriguing by far were his dreams of flight.

This is how it was done.

A BOY IN A PARK

First, he found a place to lie down and relax. Then he would imagine a ball of light rolling through his body from the soles of his feet to the wiry hair on his head. As the heat passed through his body, a sensation of weightlessness took hold. He would become so light air could slip underneath his legs and shoulders and lift him up. He would let himself rise, slowly and steadily, until at a certain point he decided to flip over and face the ground. He would look down on his body, which had remained below, eyes still shut. It was a strange, disconcerting experience, as if he had split himself in two, but unease was quickly replaced by exhilaration as he ascended further, clearing the treetops, and gazing down at the network of paths, the ruins, gardens and arcades, as if they had been laid out especially for him. But the boy rarely got that far.

Indeed, he rarely got off the ground.

His daydreams required peace and quiet and immense concentration, but the park was busy and he kept getting interrupted. Day and night, someone was always there to disturb him: from the early-morning joggers and dog walkers to lunchtime office workers to the young people who lounged with bottles and guitars long into the balmy evenings. It made him very bad-tempered.

"Go away!" he would growl at the chattering tourists, barking dogs, and burbling lovers. "Can't you see I'm trying to concentrate?"

But they would only stare at him, or laugh at him, or shake their heads, and tell him to shut up, and it was he who had to go elsewhere for peace and quiet.

One day, after yet another interruption, he stomped into the ancient ruins, muttering to himself, and promptly stubbed his toe on the edge of a stone slab. He yelped with pain and stamped on the slab as if it were to blame for his carelessness. The slab collapsed. Not immediately, not completely. First came a subterranean rumble, which sent worrying tremors through the boy's body. This was followed by a resounding, clunking thud as the slab dropped at one end. The boy lost his balance and found himself sliding into the breach that opened between the slab and the ground. He clawed the stone, long enough to let out a feeble cry of help before disappearing into the darkness.

The boy landed on a hard stone floor and lay there winded for several minutes. He winced as he rolled onto his back. He decided not to move again. A shaft of sunlight struck the wall above him. It swam with specks of dust that had lain for centuries undisturbed until the boy had made his dramatic entrance. The interior of the chamber was filled with a darkness so thick you could touch it. Nothing moved. Nothing made a sound. It was calm and quiet, insulated from the outside world. The boy smiled. He had found the perfect place in which to daydream.

He closed his eyes, and began. He used the shaft of sunlight, imagining it travelling to the floor of the chamber, scanning him, and then lifting him like a tiny, shimmering speck suspended in its beam. He emerged from the chamber into the blinding daylight. Here he turned to face the ground, but his body was no longer in view–it had remained on the floor of the chamber. But that didn't matter. He didn't need it. He climbed above the towering pines and ancient ruins, gazed down on the paths flowing with a stream of tourists, the lawns littered with sunbathers and picnickers, then he caught the breeze.

He was flying.

He flew over the terracotta rooftops of the city, marvelling at the maze of streets, alleyways, and courtyards, the traffic like tiny electric pulses across a circuit board. From above, everything seemed exact and detailed and under control. He looped around the great cathedral and passed over the railway station. The tracks splayed like the fingers of a hand as they approached the platforms. A departing train sliced through the mass of buildings. The glint of sunlight on the surface of the river caught his eye and led him into the countryside.

The boy followed the river's curving path through the blocks of greens and browns and creamy oatmeal that carpeted the valley floor. Its thread of silvery grey growing wider and darker, slowly pushing the land apart until it opened into the vast expanse of the sea.

The sea overwhelmed the boy. It spread like a blank sheet of paper, flat and featureless, to the horizon. It felt like a challenge and he immediately set out over the water. A few minutes into his quest, the boy began to fall asleep. He didn't know it was happening. Like the gliding of an aeroplane that had lost its engines, it was effortless and unhurried. He drifted lower and lower until he met the surface of the water.

And woke.

In the dark.

For a moment, the boy was confused. He rubbed his eyes, expecting everything to get brighter, but it didn't get brighter. The sun had set and only a faint light entered the chamber. When he tried to move, he remembered what had happened. He had fallen into a hole beneath the ancient ruins and he was stuck.

THE TOMB

The boy dragged himself to his feet and shouted for help. Again and again, he shouted, but his words just echoed around the chamber. He'd wanted to get away from the rest of the world, but now he wanted someone to hear him and come to his rescue. But no one heard him. Unless there was another way out, a tunnel or a door, he would be stuck down there forever.

The boy did not wait for light to return to start his search. He pressed his hands against the wall and began to inch sideways. If he kept his head close, he could make out his fingers. They trailed clammy, smears of spiders web. He came to a corner. After that, the wall seemed less solid. There were grooves between tightly-packed bricks. With a little pressure, the bricks began to shift. He got excited. There was something behind this part. He clamped his fingers around a single brick and tugged it clear from the rest, then he worked on its neighbour. With the third, the entire wall collapsed. The boy ducked as bricks tumbled down on him, followed by the massed contents of the recess behind.

Skulls, hundreds of them, together with brittle arm and leg bones, clattered and smashed on the unforgiving stone floor. He covered his ears until the deafening barrage came to an end, then crawled over the debris and pushed against the wall at the back of the recess. The stone was hard and unyielding. There was no door, no chink of light, no way out. He had discovered a crypt, a catacomb, a place for the dead. It was not a place you were meant to leave. The boy curled up among the bones and eventually slipped into an uneasy sleep.

The boy woke to the sound of scratching and, yes, the miaow of a cat. He got up and tiptoed through the broken skulls. He found the cat stuck on a ledge below the crevice. Dozens of cats roamed the ancient ruins and often disturbed the boy with their territorial fights or their demands for food and attention. But this disturbance was welcome.

"You silly thing. Have you got stuck like me?" he said. "Come on. I'll catch you."

He coaxed the cat into his arms. He held it tight and stroked its head and whispered to it. Then it wriggled away from him and immediately started to prowl the chamber. He tried to play with it. Picking up bones and sending them skittering across the floor, but it wasn't much of a game. He could only hear the sound of its claws scratching on the stone floor. He lay down and left the cat to it. He felt much better now he had company though. Calmer. He decided to make another attempt to cross the sea.

Once he was above the park, he began to move with more urgency. He sailed across the rooftops, the roads, the railway, until he picked up the river. He hurried along its course until the coast came into view. A low bank of cloud hung over the water. If he flew at this altitude, he would see nothing. He descended, passing low over cliffs and quayside, fishing boats setting out in the early morning. He heard seagulls swooping across his path, their calls like mocking laughter. But what was there to laugh at? He was flying. The breeze rippled his shirtsleeves.

But sea went on and on, an endless, textured carpet of grey, flecked with white surf, and the horizon never seemed to get any closer. The boy started to fall asleep. He drifted lower and lower until he met the surface of the water.

THE TOMB

And woke.

In half-light.

His face pressed against the dusty floor of the tomb. This time he knew immediately where he was and what had happened. He had fallen asleep again. When started to fall asleep, he would stop flying, which meant he ditched in the water and at that moment, he would wake up back in the chamber. If he wanted to escape the chamber, he would have to find a way to not fall asleep. There was no other way out, not for him, at least.

The cat padded warily along the edge of the chamber. The boy called to it and when it came close enough, he grabbed it. It tried to fight him off, but he held it tight.

"Let's see if we can get you out of here," he said. "At least one of us will escape. But you'll have to be brave. You'll have to make a big leap and keep going. Can you do that?"

He stood beneath the crevice, took a deep breath, and threw the tiny animal at the narrow ledge. It scrambled furiously, doing exactly as it was told, leaping from the ledge to the crevice and hanging on till its claws pulled it through.

The boy clapped his hands in delight. But his joy vanished almost as fast. He was alone again. In the darkness, surrounded by broken skulls and cobwebs. He was a little too young to die, he thought, and what had he achieved? Nothing, apart from flying. No one else could do that. If he was going to die, he might as well die flying. He might as well cross the sea and show he could get somewhere. And if he were to land on the opposite shore, who knows what might happen?

The boy settled on the floor below the crevice and

spread out his hands. He immediately sat up again. The soft flesh beneath his thumb had pressed against a bone fragment. It had almost drawn blood. He searched the debris and lay back down, clutching the small, jagged piece in his palm. He closed his eyes.

As he emerged from the chamber into the daylight, he felt sadness more than joy. He called out to the tourists and locals as he climbed above the pines. He waved goodbye to them. But they could neither see nor hear him. As quickly as he could, he made his way to the coast and set out across brushed surface of the ocean. It was a clear day, but the sun was sinking and its light spread with soft pinks and yellows along the horizon. He resolved to get there before it had set.

But again, within minutes, the boy began to fall asleep. It was such a pleasant sensation he almost forgot to resist. He was little more than a foot from the surface of water when he remembered the bone fragment in the palm of his hand. He squeezed. The bone pierced his skin and he started to climb once more.

The coast behind was out of sight and there was no sign of land ahead, while the setting sun had come to rest on a bank of cloud. The boy was alone above the open sea. He began to doubt himself. Was he travelling in the right direction, he wondered. Was anything awaiting him on the other side or was this to be his fate, an endless flight into the unknown?

As if to answer his question, a ship appeared in the distance. An old ship, a square-rigged frigate, cutting a steadfast line through the undulating water. The boy began to follow it. Then, as he felt sleep overtake him once more, he had an idea.

He landed on the ship.

THE TOMB

And he did not wake.

The boy roared in triumph. He had solved his problem. He had defied the sea. The great mass of water heaved and rolled beneath him, but could not touch him. He planted himself on the prow and gazed at the horizon as if he were the master of the waves.

But there was something odd about the ship. It was set fair. The sails were plump with a favourable wind. And yet it had no crew. Boards creaked, metal fixtures tapped and clanked. And yet no one came to check on them. Had it been abandoned?

"Hello," the boy called. "Anybody there?"

He moved along the deck with a growing sense of unease. A figure appeared at the wheel. A dark, hulking silhouette of a man that seemed to grow in all directions as the boy approached.

"You must be the captain," said the boy, swallowing the lump in his throat.

The Captain looked him up and down, but neither confirmed nor contradicted.

"Looks like we're making good progress," the boy tried to make conversation.

The Captain grunted dismissively.

"Sorry," the boy replied, confused at finding himself in the role of intruder. "I just wanted to ask–our destination–we're heading for the opposite coast, is that right?"

The Captain fixed him with a weighty stare and then, like a huge wave slowly rolling underneath the hull, let forth a booming, contemptuous laugh.

"The opposite coast. The other side. We'll get you where you're going, lad. You can be sure of that. We'll get you where you're going."

The Captain turned back to the wheel, leaving the boy to glare at his greasy overcoat and boots, which stank of fish gut and tobacco.

'If there had to be a captain, did he need to be so nasty and rude?' the boy grumbled to himself. His face puckered up as if he were trying to make the man disappear through the force of his will.

A dark outline appeared on the horizon. A narrow smear of pale grey.

"Is that your doing?" the Captain asked.

"Is it land?" the boy replied, excited.

The Captain grunted and stamped three times on the wooden floor. Three scrawny, mean-looking scurvies emerged from below decks. There was a crew after all.

"Storm," the Captain growled.

The boy followed as the scurvies moved along the deck battening down the hatches, fastening anything that was loose.

"Mind yourself," said one, pushing the boy out of the way.

"Don't know why we bother," muttered another as they rolled in the mainsail. "Should just let the damned thing flounder."

"Are you just going to stand there?" said another to the boy. "You could make yourself useful, eh?"

"He's the passenger, numbskull," said his mate.

"Lucky for him."

"He ain't so lucky," the scurvy replied.

"I'm travelling to the opposite coast," the boy explained. "It's not a matter of luck. It's willpower."

The first scurvy stopped what he was doing and studied the boy, then turned and addressed his mate.

"He don't have a clue. He don't have a sniff of a clue."

"Hey, sssh!" the other scurvy warned his mate. "You'll get us into trouble."

"What do you mean 'trouble'? What's wrong?" the boy asked.

"Come here," the scurvy whispered, beckoning to the boy.

When the boy stepped forward, he flashed him a shocking grin. His sallow skin and mousy hair suddenly replaced by a hollow-eyed skull. The boy's eyes widened with horror and confusion. The scurvy convulsed with laughter.

But the captain had witnessed the joke. He grabbed the scurvy by the neck and smashed his head against the mizzenmast with a sickening crunch. The scurvy slumped to the deck, blood oozing from his broken skull.

"You're on your way to the land of the dead, lad," the Captain explained. "Now are you going to behave or do we throw you in the hold?"

The boy turned to run, but the scurvies blocked his path. The scurvy with broken skull got to his feet and advanced on the boy, blood and goo trickling from the cavity. The Captain handed him a rope.

"Stow him below decks. Be quick about it," he ordered.

The scurvies tied the boy's hands and dragged him to the hold. In the brief moment they passed from the captain's sight, the first scurvy pressed close to the boy's ear, his breath rancid with decay.

"Escape," he whispered. "Escape. Else you'll never see the light of day again."

"How?" the boy replied.

"The storm," said the scurvy as he closed the hatch. "Make it worse. Make it terrible. Wreck the ship! You can do it."

The darkness of the hold reminded the boy of the tomb. He closed his eyes and hoped to find himself back there in the peace and quiet. But it didn't work. He was trapped in his own dream.

But that was the answer! He had to escape the daydream. He had to wreck the ship. The scurvy was right. It was his storm. He would make it worse.

The storm hit hard. The wind howled. The water churned. Waves crashed down on the wooden hull. The ship listed violently as if a giant hand were pressing it down. When it released, the boy was thrown abruptly to the opposite side. He cried out. Or he thought he did, but the voice he heard was not his own.

There was lull as the boy lost concentration. He peered into the dark and made out another lad. He was lying upside down and moaning. There were more, a dozen at least, strewn through the depths of the hold.

"Who are you?" the boy asked. "What are you doing here?"

"Dying. Same as you," someone muttered.

"But this is my daydream," the boy replied.

"So it's your fault, is it?" another voice called from the back.

"No. I mean, how? How can you be here?"

"Maybe dreams overlap or something. I dunno. Does it matter?" the voice explained.

The ship lifted suddenly on the side of a wave and crashed into the trough below, hurling the prisoners against the hull.

"We've got to escape," the boy declared.

"It's no use," said the nearest prisoner, his voice feeble and broken.

"Rubbish," the boy replied.

Another wave lashed the hull with a deafening boom sending them tumbling to the other side of the hold. The hatch door blew open. The boy tried to crawl toward the opening, but the incoming water pushed him back.

"The bone fragment. We can use the bone fragment."

With all the strange events on board the ship, the boy had forgotten the bone fragment in his fist. He passed the makeshift blade to his neighbour who then cut the thick strands of the rope from the boy's wrists. Once he was free, he started to untie the others.

A figure appeared at the hatch door.

"Hurry," the scurvy called above the din.

The boys climbed from the hold. They slid across the wet boards of the deck, grabbing at the rigging and railings.

The captain howled with rage.

"Get them back in the hold. Now. Or there'll be hell to pay."

"Leave them," the boy countered with more authority than he'd every thought possible.

The scurvies did not move.

"It's my ship," the boy continued.

The captain hauled himself along the rails as the ship lurched from side to side.

"Your ship, is it?" he snorted. "I'm going to dash your brains on mizzenmast. You're a dead man walking. A dirty, grinning scurvy."

The Captain loomed over the boy. He was so tall and so wide he seemed to blot out all light. But when he lunged at the boy, the boy ducked beneath his massive arms and threw himself at his ankles. The giant fell forward and the storm did the rest. As the ship rolled, he toppled over the rail into the restless waters below.

The other prisoners cheered. The scurvies cheered. But it was not finished. A moment later, a hand, huge and vengeful, gripped the rail, followed by its partner, then the captain's snarling face appeared.

"I'm coming for you, boy," he growled. "I'm coming for you."

The boy could not believe it. He had tipped the captain overboard. He had done for him and yet the monster was back. He fell to his knees and closed his eyes. Why couldn't he make it stop? Why couldn't he just fly away? Why had he landed on this damned ship?

And then he heard the splash.

He opened his eyes. The captain had gone. The scurvies stood grinning at the boy, a long pole in their hands. They had pushed the captain back into the water.

"What now, captain?" said the scurvy with the broken skull.

"Lifeboats!" the boy shouted.

The scurvies rushed to release the lifeboat. The prisoners let go of the rigging and dropped into the water beside the launch.

Seconds later, the ship hit rocks. The hull splintered as if it were made of matchsticks. It began to sink. Having done its work, the storm abated.

In the lull, the boy heard the mewling of a cat and went to investigate.

"Captain," the scurvies called to him.

"There's a cat. I can't leave the cat," the boy replied, pointing to the sea-soaked creature snagged halfway up the rigging.

The scurvies came back and helped free the cat. The boy pressed it tight against his chest.

"What its name?" he asked.

"We call him 'Bones'" the scurvies told him. "They're ain't much of him."

"Bones," the boy murmured softly as the sea pulled them under.

The boy woke with his cheek, half his forehead, and the rim of his left ear crusted with dust. His lips tasted of salt. He must have washed up on the beach of a desert island, he thought. But the rock was cold and the beach strangely quiet. No waves were breaking on the sand, no exotic birds screeched in the palm trees. He heard the mewling of cat and opened his eyes.

A shaft of sunlight struck the stone wall a few metres above his head. It swam with a thousand tiny particles. A cat perched on the edge of the crevice.

"Bones," he called. "You came back."

But the cat suddenly tensed and darted away. In its place came the barking of a dog, one of those shrill little dogs that were mostly bark. He had never been so pleased to hear that noise. The dog appeared at the crevice and started to yap at the boy.

"Help," he shouted. "Help. Down here."

He had to keep the dog from leaving, force it to make a commotion, so the owner came to investigate. He grabbed a skull and hurled it at the dog. The skull clattered back off the stone ceiling. The dog jumped back, but returned more enraged. The boy threw another and another and the dog got more and more angry and more and more ridiculous. The boy was laughing hysterically when the dog's owner found him.

After the boy was pulled from the catacomb, people made a big fuss. They wanted to know what happened: how he got down there and how he had survived.

So he told them.

He told them about his adventure. He told them he had fallen into the hole. (He didn't mention that it was he who had made the slab collapse.) He told them about the skulls and the cat who had also got stuck there. He described his flight to the coast, how he had fallen asleep and how he had used the bone fragment to stay awake, how he had landed on the ship and been captured by the evil Captain. He recounted the storm, his dramatic escape, and finally how he had rescued the cat with the strange but good-hearted scurvies as the ship sank.

He described it all with such fervour and in such detail people were amazed. Some wanted to know what really happened, others simply laughed, nobody really believed him, even when he showed them the bone fragment he'd used to save himself.

But most were entertained.

Word of the boy's adventures spread. He was asked to tell his tale many times over and as he told and retold the tale it would change and grow with new incidents and exaggerations. He dreamt up brand new adventures and people began to visit the park to hear him talk. Visitors would arrive by the coach-load and after sighing at the eternal splendour of the most beautiful park in a city renowned for its beautiful parks, they would sit and listen to the boy's tall tales and take photos of him with his cat, 'Bones'.

Indeed, this little story might also be one of those very tall tales. So if you've enjoyed it and you happen to be passing an ice-cream parlour, you might bring him a large cone with two scoops.

And if you see him with his eyes closed, please do not disturb him.

THE APPLE TREE

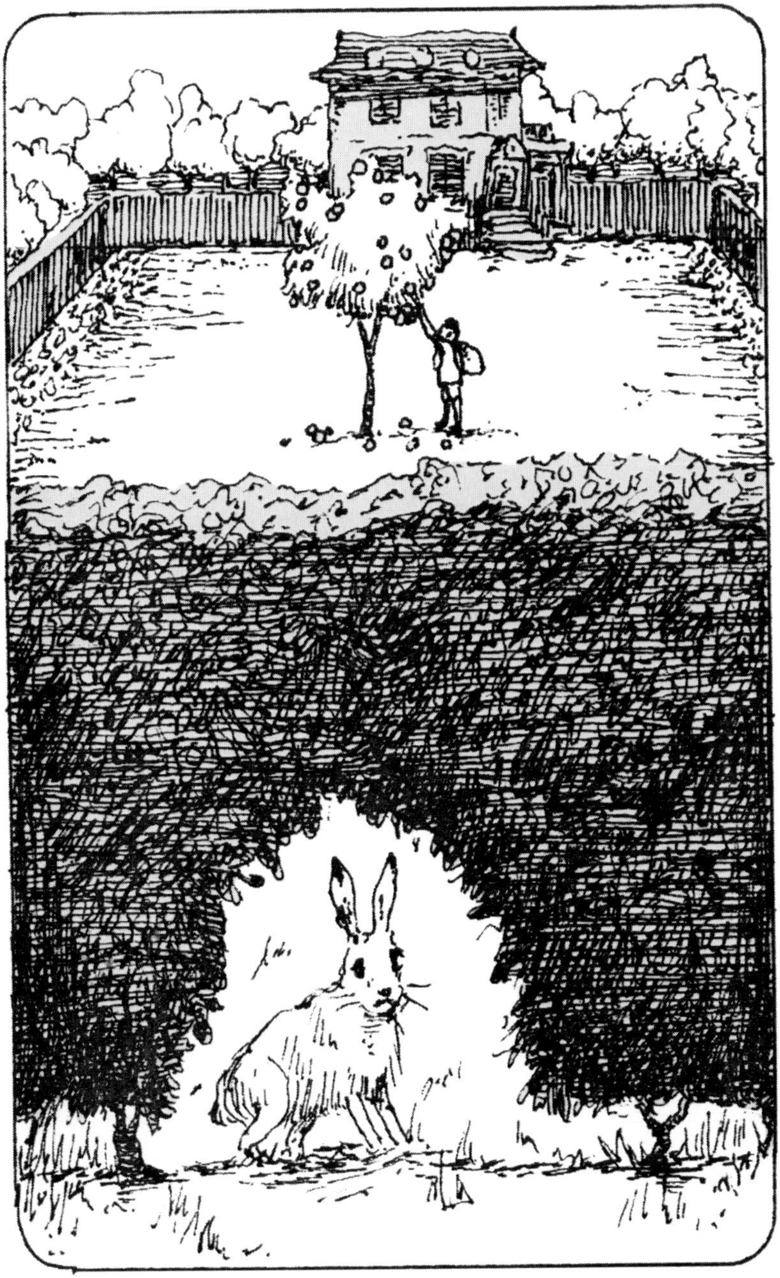

Once there was a boy who lived in a park.

It wasn't much of a park—a patchwork of unwanted fields and fraying woodland stitched together by a long tarmac path that ended, or began, at an artificial lake and a small visitors centre.

The boy came to the visitors centre to eat. Not at the counter of the café, but outside, scavenging leftovers from the picnic tables and bins. He loved to eat. He thought of nothing else. And it was surprising the stuff he managed to collect. On a good day, he might feast on pork pie and quiche lorraine, half-eaten chicken wraps and chunky cheese baguettes, cherry tomatoes, crisps, pineapple chunks and grapes in plastic tubs, the dregs of cartoned fruit juice and cans of cola. And cake. Lots of cake: chocolate brownies, flapjack, victoria sponge.

What he couldn't consume on the spot, the boy carried home to his shelter in the woods–there was always plenty of packaging to keep things fresh. Thus, on a bad day, when the weather discouraged the visitors from sitting outside, he would still have enough for several good meals.

It was on a bad weather day the boy discovered the apple tree. He decided to venture into the woods to forage for mushrooms and berries. He gathered a nice mix of wild raspberries and blackberries and found a dry place to sit and eat. After his snack, he dozed to the sound of rain dripping from the ash trees. When he stirred, the rain had stopped. A young hare crouched in front of him. It gave him a long, twitching glance before darting into the undergrowth. A few yards further off, it paused and turned around as if daring the boy to chase. He accepted the challenged.

The boy soon found he was gaining on the creature, though it would surely have been able to outrun him had it wished. The hare led him deeper into the tangled reaches of the wood. Low branches and fallen trees forced him to scramble and stoop. He lost sight of the animal, but could still hear it zig-zagging somewhere ahead.

Eventually, he pushed through to a narrow clearing alongside a thick, impenetrable hedge that was twice his height. The hare had disappeared. The boy was ready to give up when he discovered a pile of droppings that were quite fresh, judging by their glossy finish. The droppings had been deposited beside a passage beneath the tightly-knotted branches of the hedge. The passage was just big enough for a boy to squeeze through.

On the other side, he found a garden. He crawled beneath giant cabbage and pumpkin leaves, behind cane-framed runner beans and peas, and came to a group of bushes thick with gooseberries and blackcurrants. He started to eat. The sun was fresh and bright and everything was good with the world, he thought to himself, there were even morello cherries too, higher up, and beyond that an apple tree.

When the boy saw the apple tree, he stopped eating and simply gazed. The tree was a marvel. Its silver trunk, decorated with pale green lichen, seemed too thin to support the branches which reached from one side of the lawn to the other, each wreathed with sumptuous leaves and laden with shimmering golden apples. His eyes widened as he stepped forward and plucked one. He had never tasted anything like it. The bite was crisp, the flesh sweet and tangy, honeyed and buttery all at once. It was more than an apple. It was a taste of heaven. Juice trickled from his mouth. He felt giddy.

The boy quickly devoured the apple and reached for another, but a noise–a door opening with a squeak from its hinges–brought him to his senses. Someone was coming out of the house at the far end of the garden.

The boy fled. As he pushed through the gap beneath the hedge, the branches dug into his back, but he dared not cry out. He crashed and stumbled through the wood until he reached the safety of the tarmac path.

The following day the boy could think of little else but the golden apples. He could still taste the juice on his lips. He had to return to the garden. A sackful of those apples would see him through the winter. He went to the bins to fetch some plastic bags and then set out into the woods in fine spirits.

But he could not find the garden.

He tried to retrace his steps and thought he'd found the spot where he'd fallen asleep, but from there he soon passed through the woods and emerged on the far side. He tried following the edge of the wood, but did not come to the hedge. He went back and tried in the opposite direction, but no luck was to be had. He began to think it had been a dream, that there was no mysterious garden, no hedge of hazel, and no apple tree. But he felt the deep scratches on his shoulders and knew it was real.

A BOY IN A PARK

The hare had led him to the hedge. He sat down in the middle of the wood and resolved to wait until the hare appeared again, no matter how long it took. He must have fallen asleep because the next thing he knew the light had faded and rain was again dripping from the trees. If the hare had shown up, he'd missed it. He decided to go home, but had taken only a few steps when he saw the tall hedge of hazel. He had been close all this time.

The previous day, the garden had shimmered with light and colour, but today it was subdued under a blanket of mist. Moisture clung in sinuous coils around the branches of the apple tree, while the house was no more than a dark shadow in a cloud of grey. But the gloom only emphasised the radiance of the golden apples.

The boy quickly filled the first bag and was tying the handles to secure his plunder when he heard a noise. He looked around. It hadn't come from the house. The movement was somewhere in the vegetable patch. The boy laughed with relief as he caught a glimpse of the young hare, nibbling on the dark green of cabbage leaf.

"Tut-tut," he said, smiling.

"Tut-tut, indeed," came the voice of an old woman behind him.

The boy suddenly felt cold and before he could run the old woman had grabbed his wrist. He spun round, but when he saw her he immediately averted his gaze. The old woman was hideous. Her skin marred by hairy moles and warts, her jutting chin peppered with stubble, and her eyes blazed from deep sockets.

"What are you doing here?" she hissed.

"Nothing," the boy lied.

"You were stealing apples. You were stealing apples, and you didn't have the grace to ask."

The boy had not thought to ask. He never asked. He was a scavenger. He took whatever he could find. That's how it worked.

"I was hungry," he replied.

"I'm sure you're always hungry."

"Let me go, you witch," he twisted to break free, but the woman's grip was as tight as an iron clamp and she didn't intend to let go.

"I saw you yesterday," she said. "Yes, I saw you yesterday, gobbling the blackcurrants, drooling over the gooseberries. I let you have an apple, but that wasn't enough. You had to come back. And with a sack."

"I needed more than one," the boy explained. "I needed them for the winter."

"Don't your parents feed you?" the old woman scoffed.

"I don't have any parents."

The old woman moved closer. Her nostrils twitched as she inspected the boy, his bony shoulders and hollow cheeks, his hair thick with grime.

"Hmmm, there's not much of you, it's true. You're no more than a stripling, grown in bad soil, good for nothing."

"So you'll let me go," the boy countered.

"Oh, I'll let you go. But first I must think of a punishment."

"It was only a few apples."

The boy regretted his words. The old woman's anger flared again.

"Let me tell you something, you sorry little urchin. This garden is everything. My pride and joy. And this tree–I have watched it grow since it was smaller and thinner than you are now. I have fed and watered it and pruned it. I have seen it blossom. I have held its fruit. It is like a child to me. Do you think I did all that so you could come and fill your belly for the winter? Do you?"

The old woman shook the boy so violently he seemed to rattle.

"No," he admitted.

"I will let you go," she announced. "I will let you go if you promise to bring me what you love most in the world. That is fair. Do that, and I will let you have as many apples as you desire."

"But I don't know what you mean," the boy complained.

"It's very simple. Bring me what you love most, or I will come and take it from you, and you will have nothing. Do you promise?"

"I promise," said the boy.

The old woman relaxed her grip and the boy was gone, crashing and stumbling through the wood until he reached the safety of the tarmac path.

Through the night and into the next morning, the old woman's words rattled around in the boy's head. He couldn't shake them as he washed and breakfasted and went to the bins to see what he might find there. He could still feel her iron grip on his wrists too. But it was her unreasonable demand that had slipped underneath his skin and irritated him.

"Bring me what you love most in the world," he muttered. "Bring me what you love most."

What did the old woman think he had to give? Did she think he had a home and a family, books and toys, and all that kind of stuff? Or was she just being cruel?

Did she know he had nothing to give her? All he had was his shelter, his blanket, and his store of food, and he didn't love those things–those were things you didn't love–that's not what was meant by love.

And the boy was forced to admit he didn't love anything. He hadn't thought about it until that day and it made him sad. He sat at the picnic tables and watched the visitors at the artificial lake. He saw the families, the parents and grandparents taking care of the little one; he saw dogs chasing up and down around their owners; he saw lovers arrive on bicycles and caught their attentive glances and gestures. Was this what the old woman wanted? It was monstrous. Even if there was something he loved–a child, a dog, a lover–he would not bring them to the mean old woman, the witch, no matter how many apples he was offered. He could live without the apples, he told himself. And as for the promise he'd made, he didn't need to worry about that, he decided. She would never come and find him. She had only said that to scare him.

But then, one day, the old woman did come.

She stood at far side of the picnic area and was looking in his direction. He immediately ducked out of sight. When he popped up again, she had gone. He didn't want to believe it, but the uneasy, sickly feeling that had started to gnaw at his guts told him it was true and that she'd seen him. He hurried to his shelter.

Everything was just as he'd left it: his shelter concealed by a fallen tree, his blanket neatly rolled up on the wooden pallet, the broken fridge he used as a larder. He opened the fridge to check his supplies and there he found a single golden apple, radiant and beautiful, placed on top of the stack of wrapped sarnies and slices of cake.

The old woman had threatened to take what he loved most, but had instead brought a gift. The boy didn't like it. He didn't trust it. It was a message, a reminder, a temptation. He removed his food from the broken fridge and shut the door. He would not open it again, he said. But he could not resist. Every so often, he opened the door to check the apple was there, hoping to find it shrivelled and faded, but it remained as wholesome and bright as it had ever been.

And then one day, he carried the fridge to the lake, tied the door shut, and heaved it into the water. He remained for an hour, watching the surface, fearing the fridge or the apple would float miraculously to the surface. When he was satisfied it had gone, he returned home. There, on top of his neatly-rolled blanket, he discovered another golden apple.

The boy flew into a rage. He picked up the apple and hurled it into the woods, where it smashed against the trunk of a tree. Then, greedy and humiliated, he gathered the broken pieces and devoured them. The juice trickled down his chin. It wasn't fair, he said to. He had only wanted a few apples to get him through the winter. He did not deserve this torment. It had to stop. He decided to confront the old woman and beg her to release him from his promise. No, he would demand she released him. She had no right to do it.

But he could not find the garden.

He stumbled through the woods as the light faded. The spaces between the trees filled with darkness. He remembered his last visit. He knew he would get there in the end somehow. He tripped and fell, but got up again. Bramble ripped at his shins. He couldn't see where he was going. The next time he went down, he stayed down. He crawled through undergrowth until he could crawl no more and he rolled onto his back and stared at the clear night sky.

When the boy woke, it was night, but the moon had risen and its cold, sharp light laid a trail of silver for him on leaves and long grass. He followed on hands and knees until he came to the passage beneath the tightly-knotted branches of the hedge. He crawled through to the garden.

The light of the moon enchanted the apple tree, its golden fruit transformed into a monochrome silver that illuminated the curling branches. Quietened, the boy forgot about confronting the old woman and decided to collect apples instead. If he could find a bag, he would have his winter supply after all. He went to the greenhouse and returned with an old sack, then he began to harvest the apples.

The old woman stepped into the yard.

"Is that you boy?" she called.

The boy froze. He should have made a dash for the hedge, but did not want to leave the apples.

The woman came closer. The boy climbed into the lower branches of the tree.

"Have you kept your promise? Have brought me what I asked?" she called out. "No. You wouldn't sneak around under cover of darkness if you had kept your promise. You do know I can smell you?"

The boy held his breath. He could see her now. She had passed beneath the tree and was peering into the shadows at the bottom of the garden.

"Dear, oh dear. I'm imagining things again," she laughed.

She patted the trunk of the tree affectionately as she moved toward the house. And then, out of nowhere, she grabbed the boy's ankles.

"Got you," she exclaimed.

The boy tried to kick her away. He scrambled higher, but the old woman would not let go, her arms somehow snaking upwards as he climbed.

"Down you come," she said.

And down he came, landing with a sickening snap of leg bone. He passed out.

The boy was at the mercy of the old woman. Whatever she had intended, she could now enact and there was nothing he could do to prevent it. She gathered the boy in her arms—she was remarkably strong and he remarkably light–and brought him into the house.

There she began to minister to the little thief. She removed his clothes and washed his dirt-encrusted body. She made ointment for the swelling and fashioned a splint to hold his leg in place. She made up a bed for him in the basement and let him rest there.

The boy woke in the basement believing he had been imprisoned in the witch's house. He climbed out of bed and hobbled to the window. There was the greenhouse and behind it the apple tree. He hauled himself up the wooden stairs to the door. It was locked.

"Let me out," he yelled. "Let me out."

He hammered on the door until he got bored. The stairs were harder to descend than to climb and he ended in a heap at the bottom, his leg throbbing.

The old woman found him there, but he spurned her efforts to help and staggered back to bed himself.

"Silly boy," she said.

She returned with a bowl of hot soup and a hunk of bread. The boy refused it.

"You must eat," the old woman told him. "You need to build up your strength. You won't get anywhere without your strength."

"Liar," the boy retorted. "You just want to fatten me up so you can eat me."

The old woman laughed.

"If I wanted to eat you, I'd have stuffed your legs with sage and garlic and fried your brains in breadcrumbs. Your other bits I'd have kept for stew and sausages."

The boy could not tell if she was serious.

"You're the liar," he retorted. "Why else would you lure me here then? And why won't you let me go?"

"Why didn't you keep your promise? Hmmm? Answer me that."

The boy turned his back on the old woman.

"I'll escape, you know," he muttered defiantly.

"Oh, I'm sure you will, my dear, when you're good and ready."

The old woman kept the cellar door locked. She brought food three times a day and each time the boy refused it. She made porridge in the morning, soup at lunchtime, stew with dumplings in the evening. She persisted knowing he would not resist forever. And sure enough, a few days later, she found his soup dish licked clean.

The boy settled in the basement. He spent his time sleeping or pacing up and down until his leg began to ache. He would stand at the window and long for the outside world. He'd tried to open it, but it was jammed shut and the glass was thick and dirty. Besides, he knew he wouldn't get far. The old woman was right. He needed to build his strength before he could escape.

The weather turned cold. Rain and rough winds lashed the house and the boy was glad to be inside where it was safe and dry. The old woman invited him to the kitchen, to keep him warm, and put him to work. He learned to mince garlic, chop onion, peel carrots, beat eggs, tear herbs, and kneed dough. He prepared dinner every night according to her instructions and ate a large part of it himself. He forgot his fear of being fattened for the pot.

After their meal, they sat in front of the fire, the boy on a stool beside the old woman's armchair, and would stare into the glowing embers in silence.

"What can you see?" the old woman asked from time to time and the boy would answer "flames" or "burning wood" or something else that silly and obvious.

"Look again," the old woman would tell him. "There's more to see. Let the fire conjure something in your imagination."

And one night, the boy saw something. A shape began to form: two ears, two ginger-tipped ears. The young hare. The boy clapped with delight. The hare looked back at him through the flickering light and then began to run. The boy told the old woman about the young hare.

"Oh, I know about that rascal," she chuckled. "It was he who led you to the garden?"

"Yes, the first time," the boy confirmed. "I'm sorry I stole your apples."

"Only be sorry you didn't ask," the woman replied.

The boy nodded. He hadn't intended to apologise, but he felt better for having done so.

"Did you see anything in the fire?" he asked.

"Oh, I see too many things," she said cryptically.

"But what?"

"Well, just now I saw a crow," she began. "A handsome bird, clever. It was pecking at something in the long grass. Carrion. The carcass of a dead animal. It got scared, flew off, but back it soon came. To feed. There was a good meal to be had."

She squeezed the boy's shoulder.

"We've put some flesh on those bones, haven't we?" she said.

Winter brought snow that year and the garden slept under its spell. The apple tree lost its leaves and yet fruit still decorated the branches. The old woman allowed the boy outside and set him to chopping wood, though she did not let him out of her sight.

"How come there are apples in the tree?" he asked.

The old woman smiled.

"Would you like one?" she replied.

The boy nodded.

"Help yourself," she said.

The boy reached into the tree and plucked one small fruit. It was heavier than he'd expected, and warm, comforting. He imagined sinking his teeth into the crisp flesh.

"I'll keep it for later," he said, and put it in his pocket.

That night, as they stared into the fire, the boy had another vision. He saw hair the colour of flame, long tresses flowing along a girl's back as she rode her bicycle through the woods. For a second, when the log collapsed, she disappeared. The boy leaned forward eager to see her again. And there she was, smaller, further away. She had stopped pedalling and was waving to him. He waved back. He told the old woman about his vision.

"Oh, you rascal," she replied. "I can see you'll soon be leaving me, eh?"

"I don't want to leave," the boy replied.

Together they began to prepare the garden for the spring. They pulled up the old plants, turned the soil, repaired the vegetable beds and frames for the climbers, and finally the time came to plant. First came onion and cauliflower, carrots and leeks, along with marigolds, chamomile, and comfrey, and after that, lettuce, tarragon, broad beans and peas.

The boy studied the plants as they grew and asked impatiently when they would be ready to eat.

"In a while," the old woman replied. "But you'll be gone long before that day. Soon as I turn my back, you'll see."

"But I don't want to leave," the boy replied.

But the boy wasn't as sincere as he claimed. He had though of his shelter. Had it survived the winter? Had someone else moved in? The days were slowly getting warmer, he could feel it, and the birds had begun to sing and chatter in the morning. It was true he did not want to leave the old woman. She was not a witch. She had cared for him like no one else had done.

And yet leave he did.

The old woman had kept him in her sight all this time, when she hadn't kept him locked up or put him to work. She had never turned her back. But one day, when the sky was clear and blue, she left him alone in the

THE APPLE TREE

garden. The boy put down his tools and looked about him. He didn't have to leave for good, he told himself. He could always come back.

He found his shelter intact. His blanket was damp so he hung it over the branch of a tree. The waterproofing needed attention. He'd used plastic sacking, but it had slipped over the winter. He went to the visitors' centre to see what he could find.

The café was re-opening for the season and there he noticed an advert for a part-time chef. The boy cast his eye over the picnic tables and decided he didn't want to scavenge for his dinner anymore. He presented himself for the job, telling the manager how he prepared dinner at his granny's house. The manager offered him a trial as an assistant.

Of course, the boy did not go back to the old woman's house that night. Or the next. Or the night after that. He told himself he would go soon, but the longer he delayed the more difficult it became. She would be upset. How would he explain it? He should have told her he was leaving. If he'd told her, he might have been able to take some things to make his life easier, like a saucepan or a pillow. The only thing he'd brought was the small golden apple, which he placed on the side, where his fridge had once been.

One day a girl with red hair started work at the café. She reminded him of the girl from the fire. Long red tresses tied in a plait, or hidden under bicycle helmet. He smiled at her and she smiled back. When she left, he saw her climb onto her bike and speed away. The girl was very friendly and they would often talk. She teased him about his hair, which he cut himself.

One day, she asked where he lived.

"It must be nearby," she observed.

"Yes," said the boy. "I live with my grandmother. On the other side of the woods. We have a lovely garden with flowers and vegetables and an apple tree. You'd love it. The apples are special, the best you've ever tasted."

"Sounds lovely," the girl replied.

"You should come and visit," he continued.

"Maybe I will," she said.

The boy returned to his shelter dizzy with excitement. He could hardly believe he'd made the invitation and that she had accepted. The feeling of hope was intoxicating. But there was a problem. He had lied.

The next time they spoke, he asked her to take a walk with him. He brought her to his shelter, which wasn't far from the visitors' centre. This was his real home, he confessed. He didn't really live with his grandmother, not anymore. The girl didn't seem to mind. He offered her a cup of tea and while he set about building the fire, the girl found the golden apple.

It was then the boy understood what he should have done with the apples the old woman had brought him. They weren't reminders or provocations or lures. They were gifts, gifts not for him, but for whoever he most loved. Until now, there had been no one.

"Try it," he said.

"Oh my God! That's intense!" the girl exclaimed after the first bite.

The boy grinned. The juice trickled down her chin and he gently wiped it away.

"I'd like to take you to meet my granny," he said.

As he waited for the girl the following weekend, the boy realised he did not know the way to the old woman's house. He had only found the hedge by chance each time and had wondered for hours angry and despairing before that chance had arisen. But they would find a way. And if they got there, the old woman would be pleased he had finally made good on his promise.

The boy and girl tramped through the woods side by side. It was a short cut, he explained. He never used the front gate. It was too far round. The girl laughed. He was an odd character, she thought, with his choppy hair and his apples.

But after a while, they came to the narrow clearing and beyond they found the hedge of tightly-knotted hazel, with the narrow passage still visible beneath.

The moment he got to his feet, the boy knew something was wrong. The garden was not the radiant, abundant spectacle he had stumbled on that first time, nor was it as busy and joyful as he had left it. It was musty and damp and brown at the edges. Mist clung to the branches of the apple tree and the golden apples did not glow as brightly. In fact, there were more apples on the ground than in the branches. The lawn was thick with windfall and these had already begun to rot, the stench both sweet and sickly.

On the far side of the lawn, a crow was pecking at something in the wild grass. The boy recalled the old woman's vision that special night by the fire. The crow and the carrion. He squeezed the girl's hand and though he tried to look brave, he could not conceal his growing apprehension.

The crow flew off as they approached. It had been busy. The carcass was split from neck to belly and the innards already half-consumed, but the boy recognised the long ears and outstretched legs of the young hare.

But relief gave way to dread. There could only be one reason for the appalling state of the garden.

The boy rushed to the house.

"Granny," he called. "Granny."

The old woman was not in the kitchen, or the parlour. The hearth was cold. The boy called again. There was no reply. He bounded up the stairs. In the doorway of the old woman's room, he paused. She lay on her bed, deathly pale, her mouth open.

"No, no, no," he moaned and sank to his knees, burying his head in his hands.

"Is that you?" the old woman coughed.

The boy sat up and wiped his eyes.

"You're not dead."

"Not yet, my dear. Very soon. But not yet."

The boy went to her side. He took her hand. Her grip was light. He was crying.

"Tell me what to do," he said.

"You can tell me who it is you've brought with you?" the old woman asked.

The girl had come to the door.

"Come forward, child. Let me look at you."

The girl came forward and the old woman placed her hand on the girl's cheek.

"Good," she murmured, turning to the boy. "You kept your promise."

"Yes," the boy replied. "I kept my promise."

"What promise was that?" the girl asked innocently.

"Oh, nothing," the boy responded quickly.

"Nothing?" the old woman scoffed. "Don't spoil it now. I asked him once to bring me what he loved most in the world. And so he has. And for that he will be rewarded."

THE APPLE TREE

The boy went red.

"Shall I make you something to eat? Some broth?" he suggested, trying to change the subject.

"Yes, yes," the old woman smiled. "But there's one more thing you must promise to do for me."

A week later, the old woman died. The boy brought her tea and broth and sat by her side until the end. He dug a grave beside the apple tree and buried her as she had asked, next to the body of her infant daughter. He came to live at the house and devoted himself to the garden.

The girl visited regularly. They ate apples.

THE ROSE GARDEN

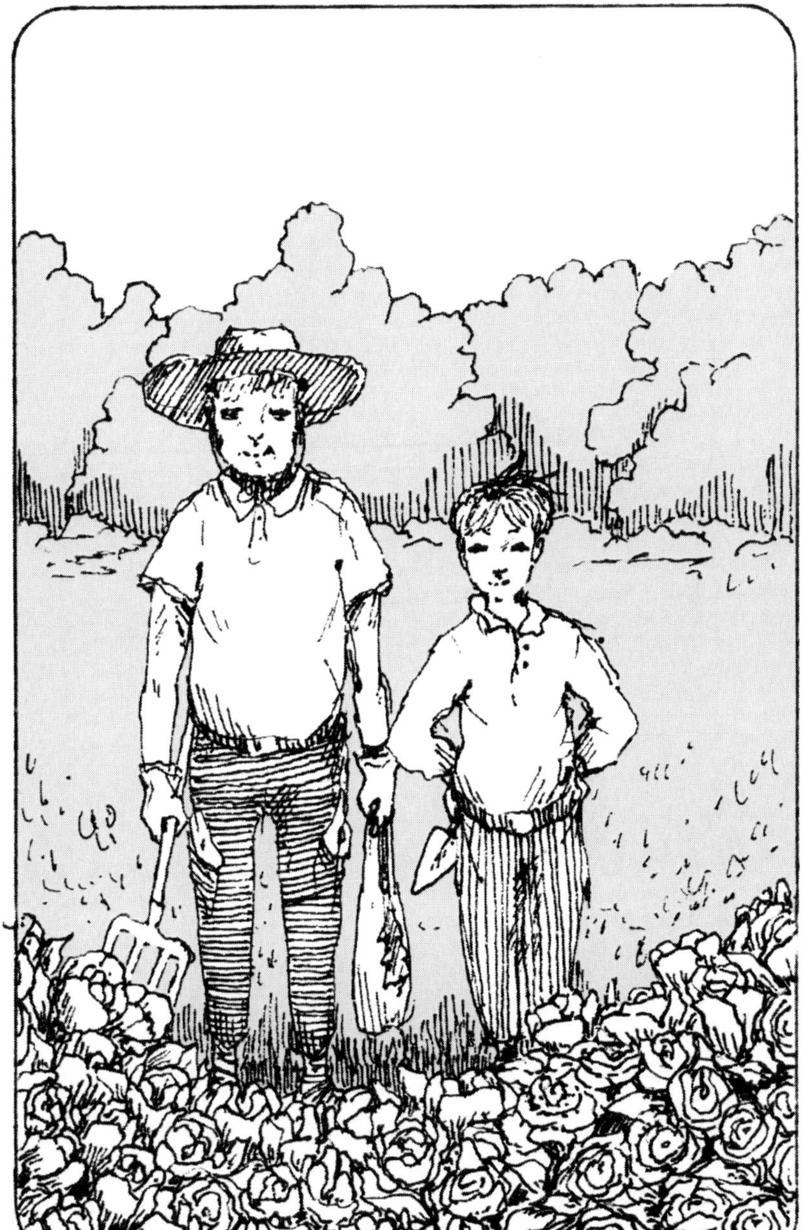

Once there was a boy who lived in a park.

It was a lovely little park, an oasis of flowers and fountains, where people sought a few minutes respite from the tumult of the city streets.

As he strolled the quiet paths, the boy–being a nice, friendly lad–would greet all of them with a smile. If he saw someone sitting on a bench alone, he would go right up and start to make conversation. He would talk about the weather and ask what they thought of the park. If they answered, he'd take a seat and ask them some more searching questions. He asked about where they called home, what they did in their lives, what their plans were. He never failed to tell them how interesting or exciting these things sounded, whether they were accountants or actors or bathroom attendants.

The boy's good manners had not been learned or taught. They were the fruit of a sweet nature and a sincere interest in people. He was very direct and after people got over their surprise, they found they shared more than they would have expected.

The boy had never once ventured beyond the limits of the park. Everything they told him, each humdrum detail, each ambivalent remark, thrummed with the promise of the world outside and as they spoke, he tried to imagine their lives, strange yet familiar, close yet out of reach.

Sometimes, albeit rarely, a visitor would ask the boy about his own life. He didn't have much to say. He lived in the park, he would tell them, pretending it was a joke, adopting a conspiratorial tone to request they kept it between themselves—otherwise, everyone would want to move in! Then he would change the subject and tell them about the flowers and shrubs and recommend they came back when the rose garden was in bloom.

Of course, no one believed the boy lived in the park, no one except for the gardeners who visited regularly to cut the grass, clear leaves and weeds, prune the bushes, dig in or dig out the annual floral displays. They saw the boy was always around. They'd discovered his den deep inside the shrubs that filled a corner of the park. They didn't mind. He offered to work alongside them. He knew just about everything there was to know about the park and could report on all aspects of repair and horticulture. The foreman found him so helpful he brought an extra pair of gloves and a set of overalls.

As they worked, the boy told them about the people he'd met. He spoke about their families, their careers, their hopes and dreams. But he had listened too well and felt too deeply and he began to confuse their lives with his own. He imagined he could do what they did, that he wanted what they wanted, and he told the gardeners about their plans as if they were his. He'd get himself a nice blue suit and work on the ninth floor of a tall building with an eye on the corner office within two or three years. Or he'd get an audition and tour the country saying clever things on stage, but when he got back home he'd find his electricity had been cut off.

The gardeners couldn't help but cast doubt on his ambitions.

"Don't you need to be able to read to be an actor?" they asked. "Aren't you a bit young to be an accountant?"

But the boy explained that an actor didn't have to read, he only needed to be able to speak and that age didn't matter for accountants as long as you could add and subtract and things like that.

The gardeners would laugh and snigger and shake their heads. The boy amused, but the foreman felt they were mocking the boy and told them to concentrate on their work.

None of them realised how serious the boy was about his plans or that their laughter made him more determined to leave. He started to ask the visitors more practical questions about what they did and where they were going. He took to following them to the gate. From there, he watched them cross the busy street and disappear into the crowd. He stood and scowled at the noise and the traffic until one day he took a deep breath and stepped across the threshold. He walked to the crossroads and stopped. There was a pedestrian crossing in either direction. He didn't know which to take. He remained on the curb while the signs turned from green to red to green and back to red again, and then he went home.

The boy was angry with himself for failing to leave. He started to spend more time on his own. He no longer approached the visitors and only smiled wistfully as they passed. The gardeners noticed something was wrong. He wasn't himself, they said. He wasn't burbling about his latest plans, the lives he was going to live. But he told them he was fine.

"You're still planning on leaving though, right?" one of them joked, and the boy assured her he would leave soon, he just hadn't made up his mind exactly where he was going to go.

And then one day, the gardeners arrived for work and the boy did not present himself. The foreman went to his den to see if he was unwell, but he found no sign of the boy. His blanket had gone. He delayed a few minutes before issuing instructions as if waiting for him to turn up. They drank tea from a flask and leant on their tools.

The boy must finally have made good on all his talk, they agreed, and they started to joke about where he had chosen to go. Had he bought that snazzy blue suit? Was he already sitting in that corner office? Was he gargling port in his dressing room? Or punching tickets on a train to Didcot Parkway? They never thought he'd leave and couldn't imagine what he'd done.

But the boy hadn't left. He'd grown tired of his old den and made his bed up high in a beech tree. He liked it there, cradled in its branches, especially when the night was clear and you could see the stars. Waking late, he'd heard the gardeners joking about him. It upset him and he didn't want to see them–they didn't take him seriously. But they were right because he had not managed to get any further than the junction at the corner of park.

After the gardeners quit for the day, the boy climbed down. He had resolved to leave. The next time they saw him would be the day he returned with a suntan in that nice blue suit and he would offer them free tickets to his show or on his flights to Malaga and Rome. Yes, he had decided. He would be a pilot. Oh, he'd like to see their faces then!

But when he got to the gate, he paused. He ought to say goodbye to the park. There was time for one last tour. He trod every path, saying goodbye to the beech trees, the horse chestnut, and the holm oak, the rhododendrons and the lilacs and other shrubs as well. He saluted the fountain and tapped each bench and waste bin as a sign of respect. The rose garden–his favourite place–he saved for last. He sat quietly on the edge of the raised beds. The bushes brimmed with tender buds of red and yellow and white and pink, tightly-wrapped in soft green leaves. They would burst into flower any day now.

It was a pity he had to leave.

But as he looked closer, he noticed greenfly massed around the base of each bud. He was horrified. The greenfly might suck the buds dry before they had a chance to bloom. The gardeners should have noticed. His face puckered with frustration. He couldn't leave the roses like that and he began to pick the greenfly off the stems.

Night fell before the job was done and the boy made his bed on a bench by the roses, intending to head out at first light.

When he woke, however, some of the buds had burst into flower. They would be magnificent. But still he had to go. He inspected each bud once more to make sure his work was done.

And by that time, the foreman had arrived. He was overjoyed to see the boy had not left.

"You're still here," he observed. "Thank God."

"Only because I had to pick greenfly off the rosebuds," the boy replied. "They were crawling with them. Didn't you notice? They could've been ruined."

The foreman smiled at the boy's reprimand.

A BOY IN A PARK

"I should've noticed, you're right. I'm afraid I was a bit distracted yesterday," he explained.

"Me too," said the boy, realising he had spent the day up in the tree and hadn't reported for work.

For a moment, the two of them stood side by side and admired the roses in silence. Joyous young blooms of sumptuous yellow, while on the wall behind the climbing roses showed in pale feathery red.

"Well," the boy began. "It's time for me to go."

"What? No. You can't go now," the foreman replied. "The roses are just beginning. You must wait until they're done."

"Maybe I'll wait," the boy conceded.

"That's the ticket," the foreman replied. "Where are you going to go, may I ask? Had you decided?"

"Oh, yes, I was going to be a pilot."

"A pilot, eh? That's exciting. But I was thinking have you ever thought about becoming a gardener?"

The boy thought for a while. He had never thought about that. He'd never asked a gardener about their lives. They didn't come to visit the park. They came to work there, like he did.

"But I am already a gardener," the boy concluded.

"Aye, that's what I mean. And you're a good one at that."

THE MAGPIE

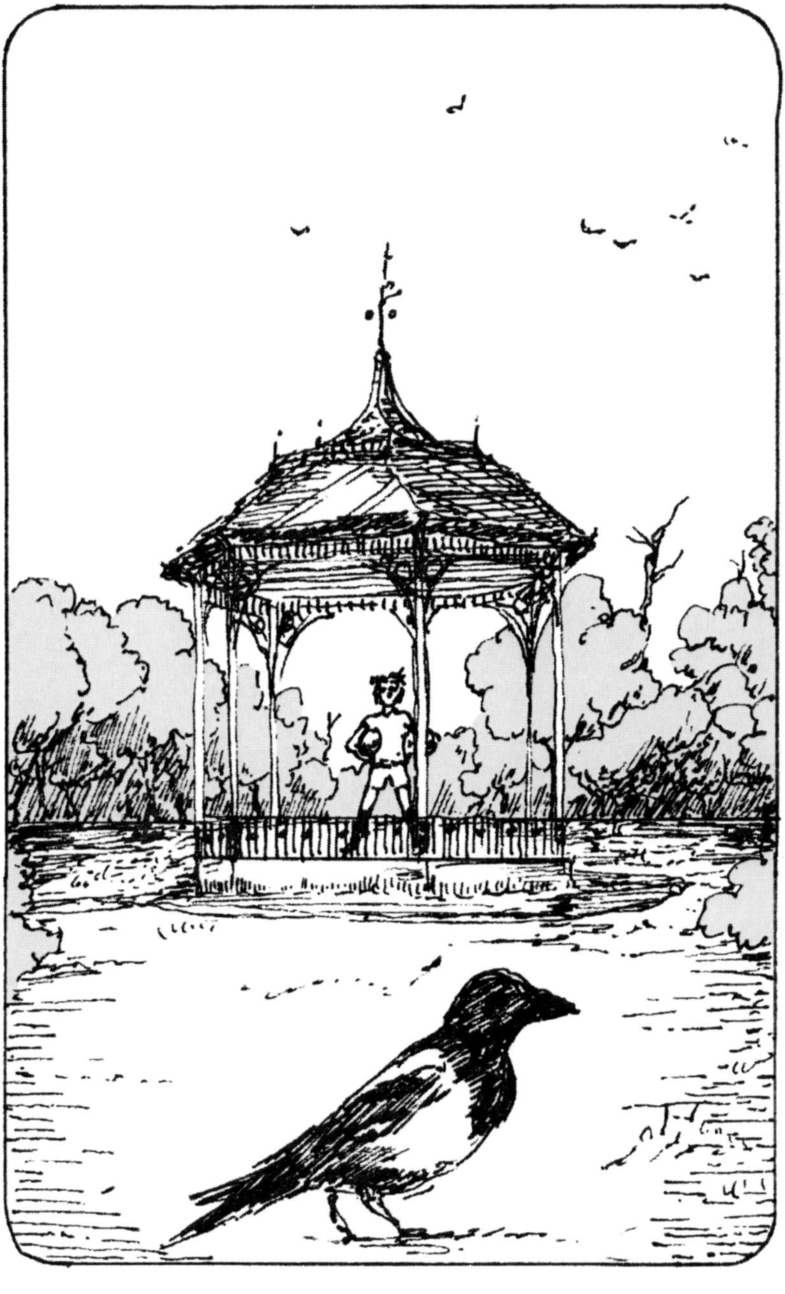

Once there was a boy who lived in a park.

It wasn't a very grand park, nor especially big, but it was pleasant and had all the amenities and features you might expect of a park. It had a duck pond, a playground, a bowling green and tennis courts, a cafe, which was closed in winter, and lots and lots of trees and grass.

And, of course, it had a bandstand.

The bandstand took pride of place. All paths seemed to lead in its direction, as if it had been the first thing built and the rest an afterthought. And yet, of all the park's facilities, it was the least used. But it was there, in a chamber beneath the raised platform, the boy had made his home.

The chamber was little more than a cavity once intended for storage but long forgotten. Dark and dirty and cramped. But the boy didn't mind. It was better than a hollowed-out bush or flimsy shelter in the woods, better than anywhere he had lived before. And, best of all, because he was the one who'd discovered it, and the only one who seemed to know about it, apart from a small congregation of bugs and spiders, the boy felt entitled to claim the entire building for himself.

It was his palace of cast-iron, cement and stone.

The boy liked the place so much he feared it would be taken from him. If someone were to discover he lived there, he was sure they would throw him out and move in themselves. He had to be careful about how he came and went. He got up early in the morning before anyone else arrived and dared not return until the last grains of daylight had settled and everyone had left the park.

Through winter, it wasn't a problem. The park didn't get many visitors and most of those were just passing through: shrunken old men hauling groceries from the shops or sweaty joggers who tangled with barking dogs and their distracted owners. But with the spring came more people: more joggers, more dog walkers, more mums and dads–or grandparents–watching little ones in the playground. People clogged the paths and filled the benches. They were everywhere. If the boy overslept, he dared not leave the bandstand, and if he got bored, or tired, while he was out, he had to wait hours before returning home.

The boy wanted to tell them all to leave or put up signs the park was closed, but he couldn't do that. (Once he'd tried to tell someone and they had laughed at him.) So, instead, he started to play little tricks on the visitors. He poked holes in shopping bags and giggled when they split and spilled their contents. He hid in the bushes and stole sandwiches, reading glasses, newspapers, anything he could get his hands on. It was a risky game, but the mischief he caused made it worth the while.

As the evenings grew lighter and warmer, kids from the local school stopped off at the park on their way home. They gathered around the skate park, on the walls opposite the play area, and even on the steps of the bandstand. When it was dry, they sprawled on the grass, snacking on chocolate bars, energy drinks, and chips from the shop across the road. Others brought footballs and started a game with makeshift goals. The game fascinated the boy and he watched from the sidelines as they charged up and down, chasing the ball, shouting, arguing, celebrating. It looked like fun, he thought, and secretly hoped to be invited to join.

But he never was.

One day, two magpies showed him another way to get involved. He spotted them stalking across the grass. He envied their confidence and watched them edge ever closer to the kids who were picnicking on the far side of the football game. They were wary but unafraid. And then they pounced. They grabbed the tub of chips and flew off. Chips rained down on the kids' outraged faces. Some were stunned, some laughed in shock, others got to their feet as if to chase the marauders.

The boy meanwhile jumped with delight. He loved it. Then he realised this was his opportunity. The footballers had been distracted and the ball lay unattended on the grass. He did not think twice and was halfway across the lawn before the kids noticed the ball had gone and that it was tucked under the boy's arm.

The kids began to chase the boy. There were a lot of them, six or seven, but the boy was fast and agile and had a head start. He leapt the hedges and flowerbeds. He swung around trees and danced along walls. He knew the park better than the kids. He knew the shortcuts and dead-ends. He kept several steps ahead, even when they split up and tried to block him off. He had never had so much fun. The kids were playing his game. And he was winning. He was better at it than they were. They must have been enjoying it too, he thought, because they had not given up. In fact, they were getting closer and the closer they got, the worse their threats became.

The boy stopped suddenly and turned to face the kids. The kids stopped too, thinking they had him cornered.

"Give us the ball," they said quite firmly.

"You couldn't catch me," the boy responded.

"Give it, or you'll regret it," came the reply.

"Here," the boy shouted as he threw the ball as high as he could and while the kids watched the ball, he scampered up a tree and out of their reach.

"See, you couldn't catch me," he taunted, giddy and exhilarated.

The kids hurled abuse at him from below, warned him not to show his face again. But the boy did want to show his face again and the threats just made it more exciting. Indeed, he wanted to play the game again right away, but the kids were already packing up to go home. It would wait till tomorrow, he decided.

Unfortunately, the weather discouraged the kids from coming to the park the next day. The boy kicked the puddles and waited. Once he would have been delighted to have the place to himself again, but things had changed.

The wet weather continued through the night and the next morning. The kids weren't going to come and the boy thought about staying inside all day, until he heard a scrabbling noise above his head. He poked his head out to investigate.

The magpies flew off as soon as he appeared. He'd guessed it was them. Maybe they'd come to invite him to play. They were his real friends. The magpies had transferred to the roof of the café, looking for scraps on the veranda. From there, they descended to the lawn, stalking the damp grass, their black and white, and blue, feathers bold in the grey light. But without the kids and their snacks, there was no mischief to be had.

So the boy decided to make some. He charged at the magpies. They half-flew, half-hopped to a spot further away. When he came again, they simply took to the air. It wasn't much of a game. They had the advantage, but the kept at it, following them across the park as they passed from tree to tree and, eventually, when they settled, he caught them up.

They moved about in the thick of the branches near the top of the tree. The boy climbed on the lowest bough and peered up. There was a nest. If he could get up there and steal an egg, then they would have game, he thought. He could have done it too if the branches hadn't got so wet and slippery with the rain.

He left the magpies and roamed the park looking for mischief. He stopped to watch the players on the tennis courts. For a while, he was distracted by the monotonous back and forth of the game. It would be more fun, he thought, if he were to steal the ball and force them to chase him, but the courts were protected by a high mesh fence and he knew he wouldn't be able to get away.

The bowling green, on the other hand, was only surrounded by a low hedge. The players rolled a small white ball across the trim grass to start the game and the boy took it as an invitation, as if they were giving it to him. He hopped the hedge, grabbed the white ball, held it up in triumph, and ran. But the bowlers were old and grumpy and didn't see the fun in the game. The boy threw the ball back in disgust.

The drunks wouldn't chase him either. He walked right up and snatched a can of extra-strong lager, but all they could muster were a few foul-mouthed lurches in his direction, which he easily dodged. He drank the lager, grimaced, burped, and walked off.

By the time the kids returned, the boy was spoiling for trouble. He watched from the shadows as they set up the goals and argued about teams. When he stepped forward, someone recognised him and warned him off, which was good, but they didn't chase him. He loitered a little further away and waited for an opportunity to grab the ball. Then he noticed the bags used as goalposts were completely unattended. The boy nipped out, seized one of the biggest bags and streaked through the middle of the game to make sure the kids saw what he was doing.

And when they saw they started to chase.

But the boy had gone too far this time. The bag contained valuables, a new phone, a wallet, a textbook. The kids chased with a ferocity they'd not shown before. The boy felt it. He tore across the park, more terrified than thrilled, crashing through flowerbeds and hedges. Dogs barked. He tripped and fell and scrambled to his feet. The kids gained on him. He reached the duck pond with the kids almost upon him. He didn't stop to face them, but dumped the bag and waded into the water, confident the kids would not dare follow him. But he was wrong. They did follow him. They'd had enough of this irritating boy.

"You're dead," they shouted as they plunged into the water.

They cornered him as he reached the island where the ducks roosted. They dragged him ashore and slapped him around the head. They pressed his face into the crusty layers of duck poo, which carpeted the ground. They let him go when the man from the boating kiosk yelled at them to stop.

A crowd gathered. They stared at this strange boy standing on the little island, soaked to the skin, hands, knees, and face caked with duck slime. The boy could see them pointing at him and whispering.

"What are you looking at?" the boy shouted. "It's my park. You're not even supposed to be here. Go away. Go on."

The boy huddled behind the bushes on the island and waited for crowd to disperse, and then he quietly waded to the bank of the pond, washing the muck from his body on the way. He retreated to the bandstand feeling very sorry for himself. But when he got there he realised it was too early to enter. He would be seen and he would lose everything.

The kids were playing football as if nothing had happened. The drunks were cackling beneath the clock tower. A dog sniffed at the steps of the bandstand, having detected the traces of duck poo. It was the only creature that seemed to know he was there.

The magpies flew down and began to strut across the grass. The boy remembered their nest. The nest would be unattended. If he stole an egg, the magpies would have to chase him. He ran to the tree and began to climb. He got more than halfway before the magpies returned. They made an awful racket. It was like the curses and threats the kids made, but worse. As he got close, they started to attack him. They lunged at him, pecking at his face and fingers. It hurt, but it wouldn't stop him. He would steal an egg, just one, and then the game would begin.

But when the boy reached the nest and peeped

over its rim, he didn't find any eggs. The eggs had already hatched. Instead, he found three magpie chicks, straining their slender, pink necks, yearning for food and attention.

"Oh," he breathed.

He wanted to hug the chicks, they were so tender and vulnerable, and he wished he'd brought them something to eat. That's what their parents had been doing when they searched the park for food, when they had stolen from the kids. It wasn't a game. It was survival.

The magpies came at him with renewed urgency and the boy, having lost his purpose, now lost his grip. He let out a strangled cry and crashed to the ground in several noisy, bruising stages. He gazed up into the tree, unable to move.

People gathered around him. Joggers and dog walkers, shrunken old men and women, parents and toddlers, tennis players, drunks, kids. They had caught him. They were going to destroy him and there was nothing he could do about it.

But the people were worried about him.

'What happened?' they asked each other.

'Is he alright?'

'Is he alive?'

'Has any one called an ambulance?'

'No, don't move him.'

'Look, he's awake. He's smiling.'

"Are you okay?" someone asked him.

When the medics arrived, they asked him questions too. His name, where his parents were. The boy pointed vaguely into the tree.

"Baby magpies," he murmured. "Little baby magpies."

THE MAGPIE

The medics asked the crowd if they knew who he was or where he lived, but nobody did. They knew he was a tearaway, a menace, but they didn't know he lived in a chamber beneath the bandstand or that the park really belonged to him.

And the boy wasn't going to tell them.

The medics slid him onto a stretcher and carried him to the ambulance.

THE YELLOW FROG

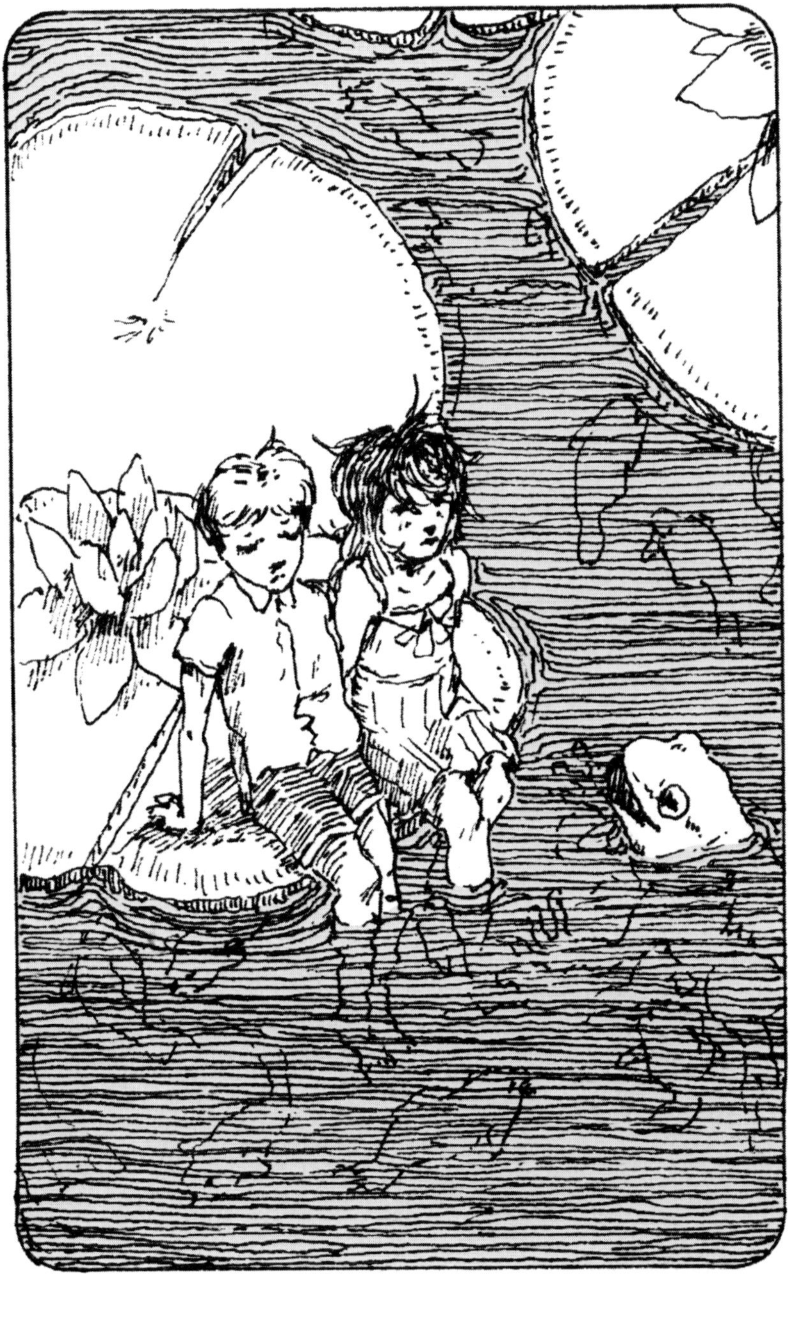

Once there was a boy who lived in a park.

The boy lived there because he had discovered a strange little shrub whose leaves, when chewed, produced a warm and fuzzy sensation that made everything smooth and good and right.

He'd found the shrub while nosing around the botanic gardens, where they grew plants and trees that had been brought from deserts and jungles and other hot places. It was no taller than he was, but thick with small succulent leaves. He'd plucked one of these leaves and nibbled on it in passing, as a child would do. Very soon a warm and fuzzy sensation began to rise through his body, from his toes to his chest, all the way to the tips of his ears. He sat down, surprised and amazed, and then he went back to the strange little bush and popped another leaf in his mouth. He spent the rest of the day lying on the ground by the side of the plant, a big, beaming smile on his face.

It was then the boy decided he would stay and live in the park. He found a place to sleep beneath a holly bush and started to scavenge meals from bins behind the nearby shops–there were several because the park was close to the centre of town. It was a dismal life really, but none of that mattered because he had the magic leaves.

He would visit the shrub first thing every morning and float through the rest of the day like a fluffy cloud on a gentle breeze. He would return at teatime and sail through the evening like a wooden ship on a moonlit ocean. He always kept a leaf or two in his pocket for emergencies. Nothing could wipe that big, beaming smile from his face.

Then one day he met the girl.

It happened on his morning visit to the shrub. He had picked a magic leaf and was about to pop it in his mouth when he heard someone approach. It was rare for anyone to visit so early in the day. He shrank into the greenery, hoping they would pass, but it was too late. A girl–about his age or a little older–stopped on the path opposite his hiding place and peered through the foliage.

"Is someone in there?" she called.

The boy held his breath as if this might somehow render him invisible.

"Why are you hiding?" the girl asked.

"Go away," he muttered to himself–if there was one time and one place he did not want to be discovered, it was this place and this moment and he was not going to give his secret up.

"Suit yourself," said the girl and she moved on.

The boy breathed a sigh of relief. Finally, he could pop the magic leaf in his mouth. Once the warm and fuzzy sensation spread through his body, from his toes to the tips of his ears, he forgot about the girl's unwelcome intrusion.

But later that day, he saw the girl again. This time

it was he who spied on her. She sat on the bank of the lake, her hand trailing in the water. She seemed sad, he thought, and lonely, and he wondered what she had been doing in the park all this time.

"Hello," he said, greeting her with his big, beaming smile.

"Oh, hello," the girl replied in a distracted, listless manner.

"What are you up to?" the boy asked, nodding at her hand in the water.

"I'm playing with the fish," the girl explained.

"Ooh, careful, there are some big ones there," the boy warned with a grin. "They'll drag you down."

"Not me. They like me," she replied.

As if to demonstrate, several chunky, brightly-coloured carp rose from the murk and began to nibble gently on her fingertips.

"See," she said.

It was true, the boy thought. The fish did like her. He gazed at the girl. Her nut brown hair was tousled and out of place.

"There's a twig," he said, pointing at a twig that was tangled in her hair.

He reached out to remove it, but the girl pulled away and dealt with the twig herself, then having been disturbed, she picked up her knapsack, swung it over her shoulder, and walked off without another word.

"Wait," he suddenly called out, surprising himself.

The girl turned and the boy came forward reaching in his pocket for a magic leaf, but his pocket was empty. He'd neglected to collect his emergency supply.

"Oh," he said. "Wait there."

He hurried to the botanic garden to fetch some more leaves.

But it began to rain. A hard, insistent rain that sent people scurrying for shelter and by the time the boy returned to the lake, the girl had wandered off. He raced around the park, from gate to gate, but she was nowhere to be seen.

The boy retreated to his favourite place in the park, beneath the low, sweeping branches of a hundred-year-old cedar. It was cool there on a summer's day and when it rained the ground stayed dry and firm longer than anywhere else. He slumped against the trunk and immediately pulled one of the fresh leaves from his pocket. This qualified as an emergency, he told himself, as he popped it in his mouth.

"What are you eating?' the girl asked.

She was there, resting on the other side of the tree trunk.

"Hey, I was looking for you!" the boy replied, scrambling around to face her.

"I had to get out of the rain," she explained. "Can I have one too, whatever it is?"

"Actually, I brought them for you," the boy said, offering the girl a leaf.

The girl studied the leaves. They were bright green and traced with deep yellow veins.

"They taste like caterpillars," the boy warned. "But they make you feel good. Really good."

"Okay," the girl said, nibbling on the leaf.

Very soon, the warm and fuzzy sensation began to spread from her toes up to her chest and all the way to the tips of her ears.

"Do you like it?" the boy asked.

"Uh-huh," the girl replied with a big, beaming smile. "Is that what you were doing in the bushes?"

"Yes, but you mustn't tell anyone else," the boy whispered. "It's a secret."

"Our secret," the girl agreed.

The two of them lay back against the trunk of the cedar and listened to the rain. After a while, the girl rummaged in her knapsack and produced a sandwich, which she tore in two pieces to share with the boy.

"Are you on a day trip?" he asked.

The girl shook her head. She had run away from home, she said, and she was never ever going back.

The boy invited the girl to stay with him. He showed her all the interesting places, the hideouts and vantage points–though he had to admit she'd already discovered two of them! He taught her what you had to do to survive. They scavenged meals from the bins behind the supermarket. They found an old curtain for a blanket and made space for her to sleep by his side beneath the holly bush. And of course, they went to visit the strange little shrub in the botanic garden.

The girl had never experienced anything as intensely comforting as the warm and fuzzy sensation of the magic leaves. She couldn't get enough. They would eat four, five, six at a time and pocket several more in case they needed top-ups during the day. Then they would teeter around the park, laughing and giggling and flop in a wondrous silence beneath the hundred-year-old cedar.

The boy thought about the girl from the moment he opened his eyes in the morning to the moment he closed them. He had never been so happy and the girl had never been so intoxicated. She forgot her troubles and thought only of the magic leaves and how good they made her feel.

And then one morning, the boy noticed how many branches of the little shrub had been stripped bare. His big, beaming smile disappeared.

"What's the matter?" asked the girl.

"Half the leaves are gone. Look," the boy replied.

"They'll grow back," she said.

"When?"

"I don't know. Next year, in the spring. That's what plants do."

"Next year?"

The boy's eyes widened with concern. Next year? Next year was another world to him.

"But what if they don't?"

"Everything will be alright. You'll see," the girl assured him and closed her eyes as the warm and fuzzy sensation spread through her body.

The boy was not convinced and slipped a leaf into his pocket. From that moment, he began to conserve leaves. He pretended to eat, but palmed them instead so they could use be stored for use later. They had to cut down their consumption, he felt, or there would be no leaves left. And when there were no more leaves, the girl would leave.

Then one day the girl caught him.

"What are you doing?" she asked. "Why aren't you eating?"

"Saving them. We don't need to eat so many at once, do we?" he suggested.

"Are you saying I'm greedy?"

"But what happens when we run out?"

"I don't know," the girl shrugged. "We'll find more. There must be other plants."

"And if we don't, you'll go back home?"

THE YELLOW FROG

"I'm never going home," the girl insisted.

That night, the boy did not sleep. He stared up at the crinkled outline of the holly bush. He had to do something. He had to find more magic leaves from somewhere. He crept from the holly bush and went to the botanic garden.

There, by the thin light of a waning moon, he began to pick leaves and flowers from other plants. He knew it was stupid and reckless, but this was how he had discovered the magic leaves in the first place. By accident. Like a small child, putting something in its mouth. Exploring. Surely one of other plants would have similar effects, he reasoned. Surely the strange little shrub wasn't the only magical plant in the world.

The other plants were difficult to eat, acrid or bitter, stringy, or gummy like sticky tape, and all they seemed to do was make him ill. His stomach turned, his head spun, his vision blurred. He stumbled from the botanic garden and found his way to the shore of the lake, where he collapsed. With his face inches from the water, he spattered the moonlit surface with fibrous lumps of vomit.

"Please," he moaned. "Please. Please."

The moan, long and low-pitched, drifted across the surface of the lake.

A moment later, fish began to approach the surface of the murky water as if responding to his call. They were coming to help him, he thought. He put his hand in the water for them to nibble on his fingers, but the fish gathered around the lumps of vomit instead.

"You're wasting your time with them," said a strange voice. It was a small voice, croaky and mocking, and it made the boy jump.

A BOY IN A PARK

A frog hopped onto the shore.

"Fish can't give you what you need," the frog continued. "Fish can't talk, you see."

The boy tried to touch the frog to confirm it was real, but it sprang from his reach and popped up on the other side of him.

"None of that," it warned.

"Are you real?" the boy asked.

"Tsch, I find that question insulting. I'm as real as you are."

"It's just–usually frogs don't talk."

"Well, I'm not your usual frog, am I? How many yellow frogs do you see about the place?"

The boy squinted at the frog. It was frog-coloured, as far as he could tell, a greenish-brown or a brownish-green, definitely not yellow.

"But you're not yellow," he said.

"Oh, really? How do you think I got my name then? Explain that."

"I don't know your name."

"It's the Yellow Frog. You're not the brightest, are you? I suppose that must be why you're vomiting by the side of a lake in the middle of the night. People don't usually do that."

"No," the boy agreed.

"So what's it to be then?" the frog continued, finally getting to the point. "You called for help. What did you want? Or are you confused about that too?"

"No, I..." the boy trailed off. He couldn't quite believe he was talking to a yellow frog by the side of the lake in the middle of the night.

"Do you want to go away and think about it and then come back with a detailed, written answer?" the frog said with mock sympathy.

The boy nodded.

"In that case, you'll get nothing. Goodbye," the frog snapped.

"Wait. Wait, don't go," the boy said.

The frog turned back.

Yet again, the boy hesitated.

"It doesn't matter," said the frog. "You don't need to tell me. I know what you want. You want to feel a warm, fuzzy sensation, like nothing could ever hurt you, and you don't ever want it to stop. That's it, isn't it?"

"Yes! Yes!" the boy clapped with delight. "How did you know?"

"Hmph, doesn't everyone? Are you ready?"

"Can you really help me?

"Of course, I can. I am the Yellow Frog."

With that, the frog leapt into the water, while the boy sat on the shore, quite befuddled by what had just occurred. A frog had spoken to him and it had promised to solve his problems. The boy laughed. It was crazy. Absurd. And as the ripples faded, he decided it had never happened.

At that moment, the frog poked its head above the surface again and let out a croak of indignation.

"You think I'm going to drop it at your feet, like I'm your servant? No, no, no, no. You have to come and find it yourself. You have to follow me."

"Into the water?"

"Into the water, under the water, beneath the water, whatever you like."

"But I can't swim," the boy confessed.

"That's not important. Just do what I do," the frog instructed. "And hold your breath until you can hold it no more."

A BOY IN A PARK

The boy stepped into the cold water, took a deep breath, and disappeared beneath the surface.

The frog led the boy to the middle of the lake and then began to descend. The water got darker and dirtier, slimy tendrils of algae caught the boy's hands and wrists. As it approached the bottom, it disturbed the sediment, sending up a cloud of muck. The boy lost sight of the frog and panicked. He thrust out his arms. One hand came up against a membrane, smooth and tense as a sheet of plastic. His other hand found the frog's webbed foot. He clung on as it pushed into the membrane, making it quiver and flex, opening a hole through which the two of them passed.

Thinking they'd reached their destination, the boy opened his mouth. The last reserves of air escaped his lungs in huge, glistening bubbles. His eyes widened in horror, first, then amazement, as the bubbles rose and he found himself rising too, gently and easily, through crystal blue water struck with sparkling shafts of sunlight.

The boy surfaced by a giant lily-pad. The frog was waiting for him.

"What is this place?" the boy asked.

"I call it home," the frog replied, swelling with pride. "Do you like it?"

"Yes," the boy smiled, a big, beaming smile.

"Come on," said the frog.

The frog really was as yellow as it had claimed, a bright, unnatural yellow, so bright the colour seemed to slip beyond its body as it leapt from pad to pad. The boy could hardly keep up as the lily-pads swayed and dipped under his weight.

"You're too heavy," the yellow frog observed. "But that will change soon enough. Soon you'll be as light as the air. Like me."

They reached the far end of the island of lily-pads. Beyond was the ocean and a horizon burning with melted butter and strawberry as the sun dipped into the water.

"Wow!" the boy exclaimed.

But there was also a sun above them. The boy looked from one to the other and then to the yellow frog.

"There are two suns," he observed.

"In fact, there are three. The third is about to rise on the other side of the island."

"But what about night time?"

"No night time here. Do you want there to be?"

"Not really," the boy replied–for him, the night had always been treacherous, cold and unpredictable.

Next the frog brought the boy to a huge lotus blossom, whose two layers of creamy, pink-tipped petals were like a smooth, super-cushioned sofa. The boy immediately climbed in and made himself comfortable.

"Is this the special flower?" he asked.

"It's all special here," the frog replied, wriggling with self-satisfaction.

"Can I eat it?"

"Help yourself."

The boy tore off a sliver of petal and dropped it onto his mouth. Within seconds, the warm and fuzzy sensation overwhelmed him. It rose from his toes to the tips of his ears like tea through an oatmeal biscuit and when it reached the top, he dissolved.

"The girl would love this," he murmured.

Some time later, the boy drifted back to his senses. He sat up abruptly. It was time to go. The girl would be looking for him. He began to tear strips from the petals and stuff them into his pockets.

"What are you doing?" the frog protested.

"I'm collecting petals."

"But why? No, no, no. You don't need to do that. You can just reach out and take whatever you want whenever you want it."

"They're not for me. They're for the girl."

"Girl? You never mentioned a girl."

"I'm sure I did. That's why I came. That's why I'm here. To find a new supply of magic leaves."

"You think you can leave?"

"Yes," the boy confirmed. "But I'll come back though," he added.

"No, no, no. You can't just come and go. It doesn't work like that."

"What should I do then?" the boy asked. "I have to go back."

"Well, why don't you bring her back here?" the frog suggested. "Wouldn't that be better? If you promise to return with the girl, I will help you get back through the membrane. What could be better, huh?"

"She would love it here," the boy agreed.

The girl discovered the boy's body sprawled on the grass. His clothes were soaking wet, while rotten weeds and algae clung to his cheeks and forehead. She assumed he was dead, but when she touched him, he began to cough and splutter.

"What happened? Where have you been?" she asked. "I looked for you everywhere."

The boy rolled onto his side. He knew something

had happened, something important, but his mind was dense and murky as if it had been squashed beneath a forest of ancient trees.

"I don't know," he answered.

The girl helped him to his feet and gave him a big hug to warm him up.

"Come on," she said. "We need to find you some dry clothes."

As she guided him away, the boy put his hand in his pocket and found the petals he'd collected in the world beneath the lake. He pulled them out. They did not have the lustre they'd once had, but he knew what they were and he began to remember where he'd been and what had happened.

"I've got something for you," he declared, offering the strips of lotus flower.

"What are they?" she asked, unimpressed.

"They're like magic leaves only better," he said. "From a flower so big you can lie on it like a sofa."

His memories had been unblocked and he blurted them so quickly and with such feverish excitement that the girl found herself quite bewildered. He leapt from one detail to another, from the crystal blue waters of the lagoon to the brilliant ocean and the suns that were always either setting or rising, then back to the yellow frog, the wish it had granted, the invitation it had made.

"We could stay there forever," he concluded.

"Stay where? Beneath the lake?" the girl asked, though she didn't want an explanation.

"Yes. You would love it there, I'm sure."

He offered her a strip of damp lotus petal.

"They're ten times better than the magic leaves."

The girl popped the gummy-looking petal into her mouth and the boy watched her expression for the signs of bliss and delight.

"How long is it supposed to take?" she asked.

"It should be instant."

The girl spat the petal into her hand.

"It doesn't work," she concluded.

The boy tried a piece himself. It didn't work.

"I don't understand. They worked before," he puzzled. "They must only work in that world. That's why the frog wouldn't fetch them for me. That's why he made me follow him. That's why we have to go there. You'd love it there, I promise."

There was a desperate, imploring look in the boy's eyes that worried the girl. He really seemed to believe he'd been to a world beneath the lake.

"It was a dream," she said. "That's all. A really nice dream."

But it didn't seem like a dream to the boy.

It was something he had lived, something wonderful, and he couldn't let it go. He talked about it all the time. It was always sunny there, he would say. Always daytime. He would describe the rich colours of the sunset and the subtle, hopeful palette of dawn, and noted how the shelter of the holly bush and the hundred-year-old cedar could not compare to the sumptuous comfort of the giant lotus flowers, while the leaves of the strange little shrub that had once seemed so precious were no more than a mild imitation of the marvellous lotus petals.

The girl let the boy talk and his boundless enthusiasm began to overcome her doubts. She had to admit she wanted it to be true. If there was something more powerful, more intoxicating than the magic leaves, she wanted to try it. But was it really possible?

"You would never have believed what the magic leaves could do if you hadn't tried them first, would you?" the boy argued. "Don't you trust me?"

"Of course, I do. But it's different. I saw where you got the leaves from."

"Well, why not come and see this place as well. Then you'll know it's true. You'll love it, I promise. You'll want to stay there forever."

The girl pursed her lips.

"What would we have to do?" she asked, unsure.

The boy explained they would have to do everything he'd done that night. Eat all those plants, vomit into the lake, summon the fish, and the yellow frog would come and lead them through the murky water. The girl agreed, though she refused to make herself sick.

"I can summon the fish without having to make myself ill," she told the boy.

That night, the boy and girl went down to the lake. A crescent moon hung low over the water. The girl let her hand trail in the dark water. One by one, large and small, the fish rose to nibble on her fingers.

Soon after, the yellow frog appeared.

"Why are you wasting your time with the fish? I told you they're of no use," it began in its croaky, self-important voice.

"Was that the yellow frog?" the girl asked.

"Who else would it be?" the frog declared.

"Are you real?" the girl continued.

"Not only am I real, but I am quite beautiful. You may kiss me if you wish."

"No, thanks," the girl laughed.

"There'll be plenty of time for that," it replied. "Did the boy tell you about the little paradise?"

"Yes," the girl confirmed. "Again and again. He wouldn't stop."

"And now you believe him?"

"I guess so."

"In that case, shall we go? Follow me close. And remember, hold your breath until you can hold it no more. Are you ready?"

The girl wasn't really ready. Who could be ready for the spectacle of a self-important, talking frog or the prospect of a trip beneath the water of lake at night?

"You're going to love it there," the boy whispered, squeezing her hand.

"Are you sure?" the girl asked.

"Oh, yes."

And the boy and girl held each others hand as they waded into the water.

The yellow frog was waiting for them when they climbed onto island of giant lily-pads.

"Welcome to your new home," it said, and then performed a back-flip, followed by a front-flip, seemingly unable to contain its delight.

The girl flopped on the floor and closed her eyes. The sunlight was warm and smooth as honey, the scent of flowers was intoxicating, and was that the murmur of a waterfall she could hear in the distance?

"It's paradise," the girl sighed.

"See, what did I tell you?" said the boy, grinning.

THE YELLOW FROG

She rolled on her side and let her hand trail in the clear water.

"Where are the fish?" she asked.

"Fish?" the frog responded, suddenly becoming serious. "Why would there be fish?"

"Because they're nice."

"Not as nice as yellow frogs," the frog countered.

"The sun's about to set," the boy interrupted. "Let's go watch."

He grabbed the girl's hand and led her to the far edge of the island where the sun was melting into the sea in a mess of butter and strawberry. The girl turned to the sun above their head, then back to the semi-circle on the horizon, just as the boy had done.

"Incredible," she said.

"I knew you'd like it," said the boy then, unable to contain himself, he ran off again.

"It's so quiet here. Where is everybody else?"

The girl turned to the yellow frog.

"Nobody else," it replied. "Just you and me and the boy. I just wanted to say how glad I am you decided to come."

"In fact, I wasn't going to come," she explained. "I didn't believe it. I thought it was a dream."

"Well, you were right. It is a dream. A dream made real, if you like."

The boy had gone to fetch strip of lotus petal for them to eat.

"Here it is," he said, proudly. "Shall we take it here?"

The yellow frog interrupted.

"I've got something better than those. I didn't want to show you until I knew you were committed. It's very special. Would you like to partake?"

"Yes, please," the two replied in unison.

The frog instructed the boy and girl to kneel. They wouldn't need their legs for this, he said. Once they were facing each other, the frog slid the two lily-pads apart to reveal a cluster of soft, transparent eggs, or spawn, with black specks in their centres.

"Wow, are those eggs?" the boy asked.

The frog did not reply. It took the strip of lotus petal, slipped an egg inside, like a taco, and with exaggerated solemnity, held it out before the boy.

"My dear new friends and companions, your lives have been full of sorrow and you have longed for a place where nothing could ever hurt you. Today your search has come to an end. You have found that special place. Partake of this sacrament and it will be yours forever. It will not get any better than this. It cannot."

The boy grabbed the taco and swallowed it whole with a grin.

"And now it's your turn," said the frog, turning to the girl. It prepared another taco and held it out for her. She took it and ate, but the moment she swallowed, she had second thoughts.

"I don't want this," she declared.

"But it's done," the frog replied.

"Well, I don't want it," the girl became more insistent. "I want to go home."

"To the park? But why?" the boy asked. "There's nothing there. We've eaten most of the magic leaves."

"No, to my parents. I want to go home."

"Oh," the boy replied, and he understood she was serious. He had feared this day. He'd feared it because he knew it would happen.

"It's too late," the yellow frog snapped. "But don't worry. Soon you will not care. Soon nothing will be able to hurt you ever again."

THE YELLOW FROG

"Throw it up. Make yourself sick," the boy urged.

The girl stuck her fingers down her throat.

"It won't work. It won't work," the yellow frog screeched, but the pitch of its voice suggested it was not convinced.

The boy shielded the girl as she tried to throw up.

"I can't do it," she said.

"You must," the boy replied.

The girl wretched and gagged and finally, pulling her hand from her mouth, she spattered the water with the contents of her upper intestine. Petals, frogspawn, a ham sandwich, and the half-digested remains of half-a-dozen magic leaves.

"You silly, silly girl," the frog wailed. "You're making a mess. That's all you are doing."

But the mess summoned the fish from the other side of the membrane and soon the water of the lagoon was darkening as the fish rushed to the surface to feed on the vomit.

"Jump," the boy shouted. "The fish will take you through. Grab the biggest one. Jump."

The girl jumped. She found the largest fish–a big, handsome pike–and hung on as it flicked its tail and immediately began to descend.

Enraged, the frog threw itself into the water to pursue the girl. But this was a mistake. The fish turned from the vomit and pounced on the smooth-skinned amphibian, tearing its yellow body to pieces.

The boy peered through the commotion, trying to catch a last glimpse of the girl, but she had already passed from sight.

The fish withdrew, while the remains of the frog sank slowly to the bottom of the lagoon and the crystal water, struck through with columns of sunlight, began to sparkle once again.

Crouching on the lily-pad, perplexed by what had happened, the boy felt his sadness evaporate in the heat. He stayed there for some time, quiet and calm, not moving, until with a big, beaming smile, he let forth a deep croak and hopped across the island to watch the hot sun melt into the ocean.

SPECIAL MENTIONS

There are people without whom this particular tree might never have borne fruit. People who watered it, pruned it, nurtured it. I'd like to extend a special thank you to JENNIFER VAUDIN and TOM HILL for reading clunky early versions of the stories, to SAL CHAFFEY for the promo shoot and proof reading, to SARAH PARKIN for advice on artwork, and JOSEPH BRADLEY HILL for bringing the remarkable artist FF WILLIAMS to my attention.

SUPPORTERS

I would like to thank the following good people for their generous contribution to the crowdfunding campaign:

PAUL ADDISON	DAVE KINGHAN
DEBORAH AGULNIK	ALISTAIR LANDELS
LARA ALBANESI	DAVID LOHFINK
RICKY BAXTER	KATH LOHFINK
KERRY BRADLEY	CHRISTINE MIDDLETON
DAVE CHAFFEY	CHRIS MILLARD
SAL CHAFFEY	RICHARD NAISH
ALISON CONEY	CHRIS O'DONNELL
NEIL CONWAY	DAVID PARKIN
JOHN COOKE	MAVIS PARKIN
BRIAN DENNESS	SARAH PARKIN
PAUL GEBBETT	AMANDA PRICE
INARA GIPSLE	VILLI RAGNARSSON
BARRY GRAHAM	DOROTHY JUNE ROBERTS
MAX HILL	SARAH SHARPE
JUDITH HOLT	MARY SIBELLAS
ROLF HOWARTH	DI TAHOURDIN
GRAHAM JOHNSON	JENNIFER VAUDIN
JANE KAYLEY-BURGESS	WILLIAM VAUDIN

This book is dedicated to my father

RICHARD PARKIN is a writer, filmmaker, and cartographer. He studied PHILOSOPHY and LITERATURE at the UNIVERSITY OF WARWICK and ACTING at BRISTOL OLD VIC THEATRE SCHOOL. He lives in Matlock, Derbyshire.

FREDERICK WILLIAMS is an artist currently living in London. He makes drawings, paintings and films set in weird yet mundane worlds caught between the medieval and the post-modern, where magic holds more logic than science and mystical sorcerers divine the Truth of things.